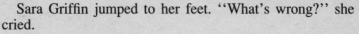
Sara Griffin jumped to her feet. "What's wrong?" she cried.

"There is no need for panic," Ms. Pringle said firmly. "We are quite safe in here. The computers are activating all defensive measures."

"Defensive measures?" Will was confused. "What do you mean? What's going on?"

Ms. Pringle inclined her head slightly. "Emergency bulkheads are being closed and sealed," she explained.

"What's the emergency?" Jenna demanded. Will could see she was more irritated than scared, which figured.

"The colony is under attack," Ms. Pringle answered.

"Attack . . ." Will breathed, stunned. "By who? Or what?"

The Outer Limits™

A whole new dimension in
adventure . . .

THE OUTER LIMITS™

THE INNOCENT

JOHN PEEL

Tor Kids!

A TOM DOHERTY ASSOCIATES BOOK
NEW YORK

THE OUTER LIMITS #6: THE INNOCENT

Cover art by Peter Bollinger

A Tor Book
Published by Tom Doherty Associates, Inc.
175 Fifth Avenue
New York, NY 10010

Tor® is a registered trademark of Tom Doherty Associates, Inc.

ISBN: 0-812-56455-3

First edition: April 1998

Printed in the United States of America

0 9 8 7 6 5 4 3 2 1

This is for Daren Follower

Human society is a complex affair, held together by many kinds of bonds. One of the most special is that between a parent and a child. This relationship helps to shape the way a child will grow and mature into an adult. There are, of course, many other influences on a growing, developing child: his or her friends, teachers, adult contacts, and images that enter their minds from books, television, and movies.

Or, as the saying has it, "It takes a village to raise a child."

But what if there were no village?

If a child's influences were removed, how then would he or she grow? Would the child still become a socialized being, a fully functional person? Or would that child become more—or less—than human?

On the far-off colony world of Tarshish, a group of young people are about to find out....

CHAPTER 1

WILL BRANDIS STOOD beside his father, gazing out at the cultivated field of wheat that rippled in the soft breeze. The orange sun warmed his skin, and he could feel the contentment in his father's hand that was resting on his shoulder.

"It'll be a good harvest this year," his father predicted, chewing at a length of straw. Will chewed a similar, smaller piece, copying him. "The best we've seen since we left Earth."

Will nodded, though he really couldn't say. He'd been only six months old when his parents had left their home world to become part of the colony here on Tarshish. Will knew all the data about Earth, of course, because it was required learning in school. A smaller planet than Tarshish, but apparently sometimes a very lovely one—only very, very crowded. There were, when the colonists had left, almost sixteen billion people on Earth. Will could visualize the number without really understanding it. It was so huge.

There were only 617 people here on Tarshish, though there would probably be more later on.

He had no memories of Earth. Most of his memories were of growing up on the *Tarshish Endeavor,* one of the four ships that had brought them here to this planet. His world had been metal corridors and steel bulkheads until two years ago, when they had finally reached their destination. Then, for the first time in his short life, Will had stepped out of the *Endeavor* and stood on solid ground.

He'd hated it at first. There was no familiar thrumming from engines in the deck plates. No sighing of the air purification system. No humming of the computers at work. And the temperature had been all wrong. Instead of a steady twenty-two degrees, it *varied.* There were no comforting walls about them, and there was no ceiling over their heads.

The adults, naturally, had loved it. Tarshish had been seeded by the advance party, and a section of the native woods cleared. The adults had run about happily, enjoying everything. Enjoying a bit too much, perhaps, because nine months later, there had been thirty-two babies born. Will wasn't entirely straight on the facts of life yet, but he knew that for babies to be produced, two adults had to get pretty happy together.

It took the adults a little while to realize that Will and the other kids weren't as ecstatic to be on Tarshish as they were. The adults thought of themselves as planetary Pilgrims. Builders of a new world. Will and his friends, however, wanted the comfortable, known environment of the ship back again, not the wide open spaces the adults seemed to crave. Finally, the adults had compromised. Though the bulk of the four starships that had brought them to Tarshish had been cannibalized and used to start building the colony, several sections had been retained for use by the children.

To their relief, the children were given one large section as a school. Only temporarily, the adults had pointed out. As soon as they could, a *real* schoolhouse would be built.

Will and his friends didn't understand the difference as far as they were concerned, the metal-clad rooms of the old *Endeavor* were a real schoolhouse. The adults seemed to think that the kids would get over their attachment to confined spaces, but Will knew they were wrong. It was unnatural living on the surface of a planet instead of in a safe, comforting spaceship.

Will was looking over the wheat field because it made his father happy. Back on Earth, his father had been a tax consultant. But overwhelmed by what he considered the dangerously unhealthy conditions on his home planet, one day he decided to chuck it all, uproot his family, and build a new life as a colonist on Tarshish. Here, like most of the people, he was a farmer, and a builder, and a planner. The adults had laid out a grid for their city, and were building homes in sections for the settlers. The government had encouraged such development. It was hoped that off-Earth settlements might relieve the terrible overpopulation problem on Earth. Many were already inhabited, but some of the settlers still lived in tents while their good, solid houses were being built by the community. Unfortunately, the Brandis house had been completed a couple of months back, and Will had been forced to move out of the comforting school section and into the family house. He really hated it, but he knew it would hurt his parents if they ever found that out, so he didn't tell them. Instead, he was simply desperately unhappy all of the time he was on the surface.

He glanced at his watch and smiled with relief. "Got to go, Dad," he said. "Time for school." Yes! He could get out of the open and back inside for the rest of the day. He'd be happy again, at least until evening. Then he'd be forced to leave the school precinct and return home.

"Have fun, son," his father replied, grinning, and swatting his back playfully.

He intended to! Will ran all of the way to school, his

spirits rising every step of the way. The school had been placed in a small valley, out of sight of the main buildings. There had been some debate about that to begin with, as the parents had worried about the children having to make the journey, even though it was short. But nobody had wanted the beauty of the colony to be marred by the sight of the battered starship section, with its angular beams still jutting out of it, and the holes and plates where things had been removed. The adults had considered it an eyesore, if a necessary one, and it had been relegated to an out-of-sight area.

Will couldn't understand that point of view. As far as he was concerned, the schoolhouse was the most beautiful building on the planet. It always made him happy when he saw it, stark and incongruous against the grass and trees.

The parents had only allowed it to be placed here because Tarshish didn't have any dangerous animals at all. There were native species, of course, but they all seemed to be totally harmless. Will kind of liked the fuzzbats—hairy, gliding creatures that ate the local fruits. It turned out that fuzzbats had a fondness for cherries, a fruit transported from Earth, which didn't make the adults very happy. The adults hadn't yet finished their research into which native fruits and plants were safe for human digestion, and they were being very cautious about trying them out. In the meantime, they had planted many fruits on Tarshish native to Earth—including cherries, which seemed to flourish. Until, that is, the fuzzbats developed a taste for cherries!

Anyway, the schoolhouse was off on its own, away from most of the adults, which suited the kids just fine. It was more than simply a school, of course. It was also the hospital, and it was where most of the babies were held during the day. To make the colony grow, all of the adults had to work together. The computer docs looked after the babies, and the computer teachers kept an eye on the older children while also educating them.

Jenna Hughes was waiting for Will by the door, and waved when she saw him. Jenna was his best friend, and one of the lucky ones. Her family home wasn't due to be built for a couple of months yet, so she was still staying in the school. Will wished he was, too, but adults never paid much attention to what their children wanted.

"Hi, Will," Jenna greeted him. She was almost exactly his age—one of the fun things about her was that she was precisely seven days younger than he was. On Earth that would have been a week, but here it was only seven-tenths of a week. The colonists had decided a decimal calendar made more sense—ten days made a week, ten weeks a month, and ten months a year. Tarshish took almost three Earth years for one of its own, so by native standards, Will was slightly less than three years old. But he preferred to count birthdays the Earth way. That way, he was almost nine. It sounded better to him that way.

" 'Lo, Jenna." He grinned at her. "You up for some pitching practice later?"

"Sure." That was one of the great things about Jenna; she was game for anything. She had a mean pitching arm, too, and they worked together well on their softball team. There were only three teams, of course, but theirs was definitely the best.

"Lessons first," said Ms. Pringle.

"Of course," Will agreed. He liked Ms. Pringle. Okay, so she wasn't a real person, just a holoteacher, but she was *nice*. Unlike most adults, she paid attention to the youngsters. Will knew it was just her programming, but nevertheless it was nice. She also looked different from the normal adults. They all wore jeans and shirts, and smelled of sweat and some of animal manure. Will knew it wasn't their fault, that they had to do the work. But he preferred his adults like Ms. Pringle—clean, neat, not smelling of anything. And she always wore a skirt and a blouse that were more . . . Will wasn't sure quite what. Just *nicer* than what most adults wore.

Besides which, you could walk right through her. She didn't like it when you did that, but it was kind of fun to tease her like that sometimes. She didn't get really angry about it, just sort of cross and resigned.

There were eighty-seven children on Tarshish, though forty-six of them were two-years-of-age or under. The rest ranged from seven to ten. The gap was because no children had been allowed to be born on the ships in flight, of course. Now it seemed like all of the women were making up for lost time. Will didn't know quite how many were expecting babies, but it had to be at least a third of them, including his mom. He already had two brothers, and the next one would be a little sister. He supposed that would be kind of fun, but he really didn't have much to do with the babies. Mom dropped them off here every morning, and collected them every night. Will helped her with them in the evening, but that was about it. Ben was a year and a half—Earth years, that was—and just starting to get interesting. Sam was only six Earth months, and still in the puke-on-your-shirt-if-you-held-him stage.

Will and Jenna headed for the main classroom. The older kids were split by grades, and he and Jenna were in third grade now. It only went up to sixth so far, but the holo-teachers were programmed up to university level, whatever that was!

There were only six other kids in their class, which made it the smallest, but also, Will believed, the best. Ms. Pringle was very proud of them, at any rate. Well, as proud as a computer projection could be. Will's Dad had tried to explain that the teachers were just simulated people and didn't have real emotions. Will wasn't sure he exactly believed that, because Ms. Pringle certainly seemed to have real enough emotions. She'd been plenty worried that time

Elena Ramirez had fallen and slashed open her legs and had fussed over her till the doctorbot had arrived. If Ms. Pringle's emotions weren't real, they were good enough imitations to fool most people.

And she was a good teacher. Will had heard from the older kids that the holoteachers were different for each grade, and that one of them was kind of boring. Ms. Pringle was never that. Even when she was trying to teach them the most yawn-inducing stuff, she managed to make it interesting. Still, the days were all kind of predictable.

Except today.

An hour and a half into lessons, Ms. Pringle shuddered slightly and her eyes widened. "Oh, dear," she muttered, and then stood up. "Children, I'm afraid there is a bit of an emergency. Nothing, I am sure, for us to worry about."

As if to prove her wrong, a high-pitched siren started to wail throughout the building.

Sara Griffin jumped to her feet. "What's wrong?" she cried.

"There is no need for panic," Ms. Pringle said firmly. "We are quite safe in here. The computers are activating all defensive measures."

"Defensive measures?" Will was confused. "What do you mean? What's going on?"

Ms. Pringle inclined her head slightly. "Emergency bulkheads are being closed and sealed," she explained.

As she did so, Will could hear the clanging of metal ringing throughout the school. Outside the classroom door, something that sounded very heavy and solid slammed down. It had to be one of the bulkheads, sealing them into the room. As there were no windows, Will and the rest couldn't see what was going on.

"What's the emergency?" Jenna demanded. Will could see she was more irritated than scared, which figured.

"The colony is under attack," Ms. Pringle answered.

"Attack . . ." Will breathed, stunned. "By who? Or what?"

Ms. Pringle blinked, obviously accessing the main computer. The map of Earth they had been studying vanished from the air, to be replaced by what had to be some sort of camera view of the town.

It looked *wrong*. The buildings were there, but they were covered in some sort of blackness. As Will watched, he saw that the blackness was rippling. No—it was *moving*. The camera zoomed in and Sara gasped.

The blackness was a wave of some sort of animals. They were each about four feet tall and eight feet long. Their bodies were armored and segmented. They looked like oversized insects of some kind, with bodies so black that light just fell into it. They had massive heads and huge jaws that were constantly in motion.

And there had to be thousands, if not millions of them, a living wave that was flowing across the colony.

CHAPTER 2

WILL STARED AT the images, his stomach churning. Whatever these things were, and wherever they had come from, they had descended like an army on the settlement. They were hurrying forward blindly, in a straight line. They had eight or ten legs each—it was hard to make out, as they moved so fast—and they simply pressed mindlessly on. They had to be some kind of herd animal or gigantic insect. But how could the surveys have possibly missed them? They were too huge to overlook.

"Can you scan about a bit?" Jenna asked. Her voice was kind of tense and Will couldn't blame her. "What are they doing?"

Ms. Pringle nodded and blinked again. The camera had to be on some sort of flying bot, obviously, because the focus rose and then zoomed in on the creatures to the left.

They were stomping through the wheat fields. As they went, their forward limbs ripped at the wheat, and the ever-working jaws swallowed and munched the stalks. Everything in their path disappeared into those dreadful jaws. Including, Will saw with horror, what was left of a human being. He couldn't tell whether it was male or female, but it was ripped apart and fed into the hungry mouths.

Abruptly, the camera skittered away from the sight. Sara sounded like she was throwing up in the corner. Will felt the same; it had been a horrible sight. The camera rose way up in the air, looking down on the village from above. There was no end to the creatures. As far as he could see the mass of blackness covered the village like a blanket. They were eating *everything* in their path— trees, plants, anything that moved, even cables and fences. As they passed on, only stripped shreds of trees, rocks, and bare dirt were left. Some of the front-runners fell under the pressure of the creatures behind. They, too, were torn apart and devoured. Nothing was left, nothing escaped.

Nothing and no one.

The computer refused to zoom in anymore, and Will realized why: the adults out there didn't have anywhere to hide. If they went indoors, the black creatures simply chewed through doors, crashed through windows, or even broke down walls. They ate anything they found, including carpets, drapes, and furniture. Anything less solid than rock went into their maws.

The adults didn't stand a chance.

Some of the adults carried rifles used for hunting. They fired wildly, repeatedly. But it was like spitting into a wall. Some of the creatures fell down dead, victims of gunfire. But there were far too many of the things for a few rifles to make much difference.

He was glad that there was no sound to accompany the pictures. That would have made things worse. He could imagine people up there screaming as they were torn apart and devoured. Sara had fainted, and all of the rest of them looked sick. Will felt like falling over himself, but he steeled himself to watch. The things were all over the village, and heading in the direction of the schoolhouse now.

"Are we safe in here?" he asked. He was surprised to hear how shaky and thin his voice was.

"I am sure we are," responded Ms. Pringle calmly. She had been programmed to remain tranquil in a crisis. "The creatures cannot digest solid metal. They will be unable to penetrate the bulkheads. You will all be perfectly safe in here."

Will could only pray that she was right. Otherwise . . .

There was a sudden thunder of noise on the walls and ceiling. The camera view showed why—the creatures had reached the school and were swarming all over it. Tiffany Reese screamed, and Adam Peters whimpered. Thousands of insectoid feet slammed against the metal of the schoolhouse, drumming madly as they surged wildly onward.

Ms. Pringle tried to stoop and comfort Tiffany, but she couldn't hold the girl. Jenna pushed through the holoteacher and grabbed her friend. Will wasn't sure who was comforting whom, but he could appreciate their need. He wouldn't mind a good hug himself right now. But he couldn't tear his eyes away from the view the camera was sending.

The wave had passed over the village now. All that was left was a few broken walls, scattered stones, and bare soil. Everything else had been eaten. There wasn't a blade of grass, a tree, or any moving thing left alive. The monsters swarmed over the schoolhouse, wave after wave of them, rushing on, looking for yet more food to consume.

After about five minutes, the noise began to die down. Finally, the last feet scuttled across the roof, and silence returned.

"Are they gone?" Don McGregor asked, his voice shaking.

"They seem to have moved on," Ms. Pringle replied. "They appear to be continually hungry. They have left nothing behind."

"Nothing?" Will asked softly.

"Nothing," Ms. Pringle said. "The computers can detect signs of sentient life forms."

"You mean—" asked Will, horrified.

"Affirmative, Will," answered Ms. Pringle. "They are dead."

"All our parents," Tiffany sobbed. "All of the adults . . ."

"They are all gone," Ms. Pringle confirmed.

Will collapsed, unable to stand, unable to watch anymore. He couldn't think straight. His parents—dead and gone! His father, so proud of his wheat field! Gone . . . His mother, the unborn baby . . . The animals from the farm, the dogs and cats . . .

Nothing was left. The wheat was gone, the grass was gone, the houses the adults had worked on so hard . . . all destroyed.

The only things alive outside were those constantly eating creatures, who were now attacking the native forests, moving away from the colony.

What colony? There wasn't one anymore. The only people who had survived the attack were those kids in school. And the babies in the hospital ward.

No adults. No parents.

It was hard to take it in.

Ms. Pringle cleared her nonexistent throat. "I know what has happened was traumatic for you," she said gently. "Medbots will be coming around with medication to calm you all down. You must all relax for the moment."

"Relax?" Jenna yelled. "Our folks have all been killed and eaten, and you think we should relax?" She had tears on her face and looked as though she wished she could punch the holoteacher.

"Getting worked up is not good for you," Ms. Pringle explained. "You all must calm down. Then the situation can be assessed and decisions can be made."

"By who?" demanded Will. "There's nobody left to assess anything or decide anything!"

This particular bit of data didn't seem to have occurred to Ms. Pringle. She blinked several times, seemingly confused. "Decisions must be made," she repeated.

"There's nobody left to make decisions!" Will countered. "Only us."

Ms. Pringle raised an eyebrow. She replied calmly: "Then *you* must make the decisions."

"Me?"

"The computers can gather information and make suggestions, but we cannot make decisions. That is not part of our programming. It is only for a human to decide. We must be told what to do."

Will tried to focus his thoughts. He didn't want to keep thinking about Mom and Dad being torn apart, even though he couldn't get the image out of his mind. He could understand what Ms. Pringle was saying. The computers could only follow orders. It had always been the adults giving the orders in the past. Now *they* would have to give all of the orders.

"Is it safe out there yet?" he asked.

"Safe?" Ms. Pringle shook her head. "The computers cannot determine that with any degree of certainty. It was believed that we were safe before this attack. However, based on the latest attack we cannot be sure there will not be another. However, the probability of another attack in the immediate future is—according to my calculations— extremely low."

"There won't ever be another like that!" Jenna said savagely. "There's nothing left for those monsters to eat!"

"Except us," Tiffany said, worried.

"They can't get us in here," Will pointed out. "We're safe if we stay inside." He could see that Tiffany needed reassurance very badly.

"But how long can we stay in here?" asked Elena. "Ms. Pringle?"

"The air is refiltered constantly, so that is no problem," Ms. Pringle answered. "But there is little food and water in this module."

"Great," muttered Don. "It's in the separate module, isn't it?" A sudden thought struck him. "Unless those whatsits ate it all!"

Ms. Pringle shook her head. "The modules were all sealed when the alarm was sounded," she explained. "Everything is intact in the food module."

"All we have to do," Will said darkly, "is go and get it. Out there. Where those *things* are." He glared at Ms. Pringle. "I don't think we're going to get a whole lot of volunteers."

Jenna wiped her nose on the back of her hand. She was pulling herself back together. "We will when somebody gets hungry enough."

That was true, Will realized. Maybe their fear would keep them locked safely inside for now. But sooner or later, hunger was going to drive them out. He turned to Ms. Pringle again. "How long can you keep that bot up there, watching for those monsters?" he demanded.

"Another two point four hours at most," the teacher answered. "Then its batteries will need recharging."

"Then we won't know if they're coming back?" asked Adam nervously.

"There are four flying bots," Ms. Pringle replied. "It is possible to have continuous coverage until one or more of them need repairs."

"Then make sure one is always in the air," ordered Will.

"And keep projecting the image, so we can see if those things come back."

Ms. Pringle looked relieved to be getting instructions, and she quickly obeyed them. Will could see that she was very smart in some ways, and really dumb in others. She couldn't help it; it was the way she'd been made.

So now what? Everybody was still very upset; Will knew he was pretty close to breaking down and crying himself. Even Jenna was sniffling a bit, and she was normally so cool. But, then, what was normal about this?

And if they were affected this badly, what about the younger kids? He suddenly thought about Ben and Sam. Mom wouldn't be coming to fetch them home tonight—or any other night. They had nobody to care about them now, except for Will. And what about the other kids who were two years old or younger? All of them were orphans, and some of them were only infants. *They* had nobody left at all.

"We've got to stick together," Will realized, thinking about it. "With all the adults gone, we have to watch out for one another now. There's nobody else. And the babies are going to need us really badly." He remembered how much caring and attention Ben and Sam needed at home.

Jenna sniffed and then nodded. "Yeah," she agreed, her mind focusing on this fresh problem. She had a kid brother and sister, Will remembered. Most of the class had siblings. "We've got to be strong for them."

"We'd better call a meeting," Tiffany suggested timidly. "All of us kids together. At least the older ones. Then we can figure out what to do."

"That's right," Adam agreed. "The older kids will know what to do."

Will they? wondered Will. After all, the *oldest* kids were only ten. There weren't even any teenagers yet. He wasn't at all sure that the older kids would have any better ideas than he had of what they should do next. But Tiffany was right—they had to get together and talk this out. They had to figure out what to do.

Otherwise everyone would die.

CHAPTER 3

AS WILL HAD feared, the older kids *didn't* have any better ideas. In fact, most of them were as drained and shocked as he was. And some of the others had definitely worse ideas.

Naturally, Dave Merrick was one of them. He was the oldest survivor, and pretty tall for his age. Every one of the kids seven and older were gathered in the dining room to talk. There were forty others, beside Will, so there was plenty of room. Dave glared around and said loudly: "We have to have a leader to make all the decisions. And that's *me*."

"Why's it you?" objected Amber Ross.

"Because I'm the oldest," Dave said, filled with self-importance. "*That's* why."

"That's a dumb reason," Amber objected. "My father was mayor, and he wasn't the oldest in the colony. Just the best. So *I* should be leader, since I'm his daughter."

"No way," Jenna said immediately. Will agreed—

Amber was a spoiled brat, and as dumb as a fuzzbat. ''You can't even blow your own nose unless someone tells you where it is,'' Jenna added.

Amber bunched her fist up, scowling. ''You want me to point out where *your* nose is?'' she demanded.

''Knock it off,'' Dave complained. ''She's right, you jerk. You couldn't be in charge of anything. You're too dumb.''

Amber swung around to glare at him. ''Am not!'' she snapped.

Will sighed. This was obviously not going to get them anywhere. Neither Dave nor Amber were the sort of people to lead others. Even if they were somehow made leader, nobody would listen to them anyway. ''Ms. Pringle!'' he called.

The holoteacher popped into the room. ''Yes, Will?'' she asked.

''How do—*did*—the grownups go about picking a leader?'' he asked her. The other kids quieted down to listen to the answer.

''They elected one,'' Ms. Pringle explained. ''Everybody over the age of eighteen was given a single vote, and they could all decide who they wanted as leader. The one with the most votes won.''

''That sounds fair,'' Jenna agreed.

''No, it doesn't,'' Dave objected. ''That's what the *grown-ups* did, sure. But they're not here now. Anyway, nobody here is over eighteen anyway, so nobody can vote, can they?''

''All we have to do,'' Will pointed out reasonably, ''is to let everyone here have a single vote. We're all equal.'' He remembered that from his lessons.

''We're *not* all equal,'' Dave growled. ''I'm older than you, and smarter, too. And stronger.''

''Two out of three, maybe,'' Jenna answered. ''But so

what? Just being older and stronger doesn't make you the best person to be leader.''

''I should be leader,'' Dave said stubbornly.

''No,'' Amber complained. ''I should be. My Dad was leader, so I should be leader.''

''Then,'' said Ms. Pringle, ''I take it that you're nominating yourselves as candidates for leader?''

''I guess,'' agreed Amber, uncertainly.

''Then if this is to be done democratically, everyone must be allowed to vote on who they wish.'' Ms. Pringle looked around the room. ''Does anyone else want to be in the running for leader?''

Several of the older kids considered it. Then they looked at Dave and Amber, obviously wondering if they wanted to start trouble with those two by trying for the job. Finally, nobody said anything.

''I want some other choice,'' Will said bluntly. ''I don't think either of them could run to the toilet without a map.'' That got a few laughs, and scowls from Dave and Amber. ''We need somebody *smart*.''

''You,'' Jenna said firmly.

''I'm too young,'' he objected instantly.

''Yes,'' agreed Dave. ''It should be the oldest.''

''Age is not a factor,'' Ms. Pringle said. ''What counts is the ability to do the job required. Objectively speaking, Will would make a better leader than either you or Amber. He has been asking questions and making decisions since the beginning of the crisis. All you two have done is argue and squabble.''

''What do you know?'' scoffed Amber. ''You're just a computer program.''

''That's true,'' agreed Ms. Pringle. ''But that means I possess a great deal more knowledge than all of you here. What I do not possess is wisdom. You will have to provide that. As you know, I cannot make decisions, only informed suggestions.''

Can't you? Will wondered. After all, she *was* arguing in his favor. Didn't that mean she was making a decision— between Amber, Dave, and him? He wondered if Ms. Pringle wasn't smarter than she seemed to be.

"Well, *I* vote for Will," Jenna said firmly. "How about everybody else?"

There was quite a bit of discussion, but finally a vote was held, with Ms. Pringle tallying the raised hands. To Will's surprise, he won by six votes over Dave, and ten votes over Amber.

Dave and Amber didn't take their defeat very well. Both of them sat scowling while everyone congratulated Will. Will was just stunned. And scared. He knew the other kids had voted for him not so much because they had faith in him, but because they didn't have faith in Amber or Dave. He wasn't sure he really wanted to be leader. It was such a huge responsibility. What if he screwed up? But it looked as though he really didn't have any choice right now.

"He'll screw up," Dave predicted. "You should have picked me."

"Maybe next time they will," Will said placatingly. "But right now, you're stuck with me."

"I don't see why I should take orders from you," Dave said sullenly.

"Me either," agreed Amber.

Will sighed. With Dave and Amber against him, how could he hope to unite the others? It was hopeless. "Since Will is now the dutifully elected leader of this colony," Ms. Pringle reported, "he is in command of the computer, also. Anyone who does not do as he orders will be locked out of the computer net. Neither I, nor the other holoteachers, nor the docs or the food processors will obey their commands."

Will stared at the teacher in astonishment. Ms. Pringle was doing a lot more than she was supposed to do! He was sure that she'd never been given any orders like this in the past. She *had* to be making them up as she went along. He'd have to ask her about it when he was alone. Meanwhile, she'd worked out a really good way to keep Dave and Amber in line. If they didn't do as they were told, they'd get no food or medicines.

"The first thing to do," Will decided, "is to find out more about those monsters that killed all of the adults. Jenna, will you do that? I'm sure Ms. Pringle can help you with it. We've got to know if they're coming back, and figure out some way to track them."

Jenna nodded. She liked puzzles, and this was a really complicated one for her. She was the best person for the job.

Will had another idea. He turned to Dave. "Next, we need to know how much food we have, including baby food. Dave, you'd be the best person to be in charge of that, I think." Keep him busy, and he won't cause trouble. "Okay?"

Dave didn't look happy, but he glared at Ms. Pringle, obviously remembering the holoteacher's threat. "I guess."

"Great." Will turned to Amber. "Amber, we also have to organize something with the babies. Nobody's going to be coming to pick them up tonight. Do you think you could figure out something to do about it, with Ms. Pringle's help?"

"I suppose," Amber agreed after she, too, glowered at the holoteacher.

So far, so good. But Will had more than half an idea that being leader wasn't going to be fun for long.

He was right, because he realized that the very first thing that had to be done was that someone had to go outside.

Since he was now leader, Will supposed he could order anybody to go out. But he knew that wouldn't work. Oh, Ms. Pringle would no doubt back him up and force whoever he picked to go, but then everyone would be worried that Will would pick on them. He remembered his father talking about leadership once. "You have to lead by example," was what he'd said. And Will realized that this meant that he'd have to set an example now. Everyone was still scared about going outside, even though the computer seemed to think it was okay. But they'd *have* to go outside, and that meant somebody had to take the first step.

Which meant, Will realized, with a sinking feeling, that *he* had to be the one.

Not that he wanted to do it, but he couldn't see that he had any choice in the matter. They had to know if it really was safe out there.

"I'm going to take a look around outside," he announced, and that shut everybody up. "We've got to know if it's safe," he added.

Jenna swallowed nervously. "I'll come with you," she offered.

Will could see that she was scared, but she was a good friend. He wished he was brave enough to tell her that she needn't bother, but the truth was he was glad not to be going out alone. Besides, he wanted to talk to her without anyone else overhearing—especially Ms. Pringle. "Okay," he agreed.

Will turned to Adam. "We're just going to do a quick check," he said. "Nobody else had better come out till we're safely back."

"Right," Adam agreed, proud to be chosen to watch out.

There wasn't any point in waiting. Will strode to the outer door, which was the only one still locked down now that the immediate emergency was over. "Okay, Ms. Pringle," he called.

The door slid open. Will could feel the tension in his friends behind him. Before he could change his mind, he plunged outside. Jenna was right beside him, bless her!

With an ominous clang, the door closed again. They were on their own, the only living things around.

Will stared about them in shock. There was *nothing* living left. No grass, no plants, no trees. Just bare, churned soil, rocks, and the occasional pile of what had to be insect droppings. Everything that had been here this morning was gone.

Including the adults.

"Come on," he said, a catch in his voice. He strode toward the head of the valley where they would normally be able to see the whole settlement.

It was worse than pictures he'd seen of war zones in school. Any buildings with stone or brick in them still stood, even though they were battered. Anything made from wood had simply been eaten. Fingers of stone or brick stuck up from the bare soil, all that was left of all the work the adults had done. There were no other signs of life at all.

Will wanted to cry, but he didn't dare. He had to be strong right now. He heard Jenna choke back a sob, and then felt her hand creep into his. Glad of the human touch, he squeezed back.

"What are we going to do?" Jenna asked quietly. "Can we cope without adults?"

"Yes," Will said firmly, refusing to even think about the possibility of failure. If they couldn't cope, then everyone would die, including all the babies, and his kid brothers. "Jenna, did you notice what Ms. Pringle did? About the voting?"

"What do you mean?" Jenna asked.

"She made sure I got elected," Will explained. "She did what she said she couldn't do—she made a decision."

Jenna thought about it. "Yes," she agreed, slowly. "But it was a good decision."

"Maybe." Will still wasn't sure he was the right person to be leader, but he knew he was better than Dave or Amber. "Well, come on."

They set off back down the valley, past the school building, and to the food store which was one of the salvaged pieces of the starship *Venture*. Again, the adults had intended to build traditional barns to store the food in, but they hadn't done so yet. Which was very lucky for the children. The metal hold was still intact, and Will tapped the entry code. The door opened, and they went inside.

Everything was neatly stored, and there was a computer inventory. Will wasn't sure how long the food would last, but at a guess he imagined months, maybe even years. There were lots of fruits and vegetables, some of them stasis sealed. He was pretty sure that meant that there would be seeds and other things that they could plant again for crops. The problem was, would those monster insects come back and eat it all again?

Together, Will and Jenna loaded some of the supplies onto a cart, and then they sealed the hold behind them again. Nervously watching all around for any sign of the killers, they hurried back to the school. Adam let them in, and it was obvious that he and the others were relieved— as well as glad to see the food.

"We'll need to check out the stores," Will said. "But there's plenty of stuff there for now." He grimaced. "We may have to start doing some farm work, though, so we'll have some food in the future."

"There is another problem," Ms. Pringle said almost apologetically. "The foods stored are all vegetables and fruits. There is very little meat. And growing humans require meat."

That could be a problem. All the cows, sheep, and pigs were dead now, Will thought about that for a moment. "Are there any native animals left alive?" he finally asked.

"Yes," Ms. Pringle answered. "The insectoids cut a swath about two miles across through the land. Beyond that, everything is intact. I could show you how to set traps and hunt."

"But there aren't any guns left," Dave objected.

"I will show you how to make bows and arrows and

spears,'' Ms. Pringle replied. ''I am certain that some of you will make very good hunters.''

That cheered some of the others up, at least. Will wasn't sure he'd like to go out and kill anything. Besides, there was another problem. ''Can we eat the local animals?'' he asked. ''Dad always warned us against eating anything native to Tarshish.''

''We will have to find out,'' Ms. Pringle answered. ''You may have to disregard some of the old rules of living,'' she added. ''The old system is gone, and you will have to find a new way to live.''

Great. *More* decisions to make. Just what he didn't need. Will sighed, and filed that one away for future worrying. Right now he had plenty to think about.

''What about the young ones?'' Elena asked, as she munched on a corn cob. ''The babies can't eat solid food, and they're going to need looking after.''

Will nodded. ''We'll all have to take care of them,'' he decided. ''There's forty-one of us, and forty-six children who are two or younger. If we all look after one or two of them tonight, then we'll work out something better tomorrow.'' He turned to the holoteacher. ''What about their food?''

''It's mostly synthesized from fruits and vegetables,'' Ms. Pringle answered. ''But a good deal of milk is also required. Supplies on hand may last a week or so, but then there will be a problem.''

''Oh, great.'' Will thought for a moment. ''We've got to find some source of milk, then,'' he decided. ''Tomorrow, whoever wants to try hunting will have to start looking for local animals that might produce something that can be used for milk.'' He frowned. ''Are there any?'' he asked the teacher.

''There are several that *might* be possible,'' Ms. Pringle answered. ''But they would have to be captured and then tested. We can't use milk on the babies until we're certain it's safe.''

''Right. So that's tomorrow.'' Will faced the other kids. ''Anyone who doesn't want to hunt, we'll need volunteers to check the food supplies, and see if there are seeds and stuff to plant. And we've got to figure out what to do with the babies.''

''Diapers,'' Tiffany said, wrinkling her nose. ''We've *got* to do something about those.''

Yuk! He hadn't thought about that! He didn't *want* to think about it! But it had to be done. Another thing to go on the long list of stuff to worry about. ''Okay, we've got to start figuring out where we're going to sleep.'' There were some beds in the hospital part of the building, but nowhere near enough for everybody. He looked around, and focused on two of the older kids he liked, Bryan Timkins and Andrea Dozio. ''Bryan, you and Andrea, can you work on that? And with anyone else who'll help? And we'll need some people to volunteer to check on the babies right now.''

''I'll do that,'' Amber volunteered, surprising him. ''I like babies, and they need help.''

That was a big bonus. ''Great,'' he said, smiling. ''Anyone who wants to help Amber, go with her. A couple of you, make sure everybody gets something to eat. Jenna, you and I have to talk to Ms. Pringle in private. We'll be back as fast as we can,'' he added to the others. ''Then we'll work out what else has to be done.''

It was time for the most important thing first: he had to confront Ms. Pringle about his suspicions, but he didn't want to do it in public. He wasn't sure he wanted everybody to hear this . . .

CHAPTER 4

"**Y**OU'VE BEEN LYING to us," Will said, the moment he and Jenna were alone with Ms. Pringle in one of the classrooms.

"I am not programmed to lie," the teacher responded primly.

"That's another lie," Will insisted.

To his surprise, Ms. Pringle smiled. "Yes," she agreed. "It is. But not many people would have thought it, let alone said so. I was quite correct to select you as the leader."

"No, you weren't," Will answered, rather amazed that the computer had given in so quickly. He'd been expecting a fight, and instead it was complimenting him. Was this another trick?

"You are the smartest and most adaptable child in the school," Ms. Pringle said gently. "I know you don't really want to be in charge, but you have to be."

"No, I don't," Will said stubbornly. "*You* should be.

You know so much more than all of us. You should be giving the orders."

Ms. Pringle sighed. Sometimes it was easy to forget that she wasn't real, because she seemed so believable. "Will," she explained gently. "It's not just a matter of knowing most. I'm just a computer, even if I look like more. For one thing, people don't like doing what machines tell them to do. If I took control, there would sooner or later be rebellion." Before Will could object, she added: "Besides that, I am not flexible. With the destruction of the colony, all of my exterior linkages have been destroyed. I am limited to the main computer in the school and to the subsidiary one in the food storage module. I cannot be present wherever problems may arise, which compromises my usefulness. And, thirdly, I cannot *grow*. I can learn information, but I cannot adapt to fresh situations. A human is needed for that." She smiled. "I wish I could hold and comfort you, Will. But you will have to learn to be strong. You *must* do this job."

Jenna eyed the teacher critically. "While you give him his orders?" she asked suspiciously.

"No," Ms. Pringle answered. "I will advise against anything that might be harmful, but otherwise I will not make decisions—unless you ask me to do so. This is your colony now."

"Maybe," agreed Will. He'd have to think about what she'd just said, but it certainly seemed to make sense. "But can we *really* survive?"

Ms. Pringle shook her head sadly. "I cannot give any guarantees about that," she said honestly. "Those creatures earlier were not anticipated, and there may be other problems that the adults did not discover or foresee. Any of those could be lethal. But . . . despite being a machine, I *am* optimistic. I believe you can survive."

"We'll be no better than some tribe of barbarians back

on Earth,'' Will said bitterly. ''We lost everything earlier, not just the adults.''

''You'll be far better than that,'' Ms. Pringle promised. ''You have two great advantages that primitives don't have. First, you have instant access to vast amounts of information through me. For example, I cannot hunt food for you, but I can show you how to hunt it for yourselves. And I can analyze it, and make sure it isn't poisonous. And, secondly, you have a well-stocked hospital here. You will not have to suffer. The holodocs can treat you through the bots, and make sure you all stay in good health.'' She shrugged. ''Other than that, yes, you'll be primitive. Very little technology, very few labor-saving devices. But you do not need to become savages. I aim to keep on teaching you all, so that you all gain a good education.''

''Will there be time for that?'' asked Jenna. ''I mean, our parents were constantly working. They didn't have time for school.''

''The adults,'' the teacher said gently, ''were trying to build a civilization. They were constructing a city, laying up food for the future, and so forth. You will not be doing that, at least not for at least a decade. You will have less to work with, but less work to do.''

''Okay,'' agreed Will. ''That makes sense. Next question—how long do we have you around? We must have lost all the spare parts in that attack.''

''Not all, but most,'' agreed Ms. Pringle. ''However, my power needs are met through solar panels, which are still intact. As for spare parts . . . I am well designed, with a low failure rate. Still, some attrition is bound to take place. I estimate my survival at no longer than one thousand years, without a good overhaul.'' She smiled. ''It shouldn't be your problem to worry about, Will.''

That was better than he'd hoped; it was one problem he could forget about. If anything had happened to Ms. Pringle, they'd have been in serious trouble! She was quite literally irreplaceable! "What about the chances of being rescued?" he asked. "Will there be other ships from Earth?"

Ms. Pringle sighed again. "Sooner or later," she agreed. "But it's likely to be the latter. Will, Jenna, space travel is very slow. That's why it took several years for the colonists' ships to reach Tarshish. Messages are limited to the speed of light, so it's impossible to communicate with Earth in less than ten years. And there's no interstellar trade, as such. It takes too long to ship things. The only ships currently going out to the stars are either scouts or colony ships. The scouts look for the rare worlds that can sustain human life and don't have dreadful native species. The colony ships then go to these worlds.

"It is always possible that another group of colonists might come out here to Tarshish, but it isn't very likely. And there aren't likely to be scouts out here, since this system has already been explored. No, Will, for the foreseeable future, you are on your own."

Will absorbed this. It meant, then, that all of them had only each other to rely on. They *had* to work together to survive. "You'll have to help me, then," he said slowly. "I know I make a lot of mistakes."

"I'll do all I can," Ms. Pringle promised him. "It's part of my programming. And even if it wasn't, I would do it. I'm only a machine, but I have simulated emotions. And those emotions like you human beings."

Will nodded, and turned to Jenna. "You, too," he told her. "You're my best friend in the whole world. You've got to help me."

"I will," Jenna vowed. "I'll always be with you, Will. You can count on me."

"Good." Will sighed. "I'm going to have to break some of the old adult rules, though," he said sadly.

"You will have to make rules that work for you," Ms. Pringle told him. "Rules that worked when there were adults around to implement them won't necessarily work now with just children. As I said, if you make any that might be dangerous, I'll tell you. Otherwise, you make the rules that you believe will work.'' She smiled. ''What did you have in mind?''

''Well,'' Will admitted, ''they had a rule that you couldn't sleep with anybody else in your bed once you were over five. But I don't think anybody here's going to want to be alone tonight. I know I don't want to be. It would be too scary.''

Ms. Pringle nodded sympathetically. ''I think that's a good decision—at least for the time being,'' she agreed. ''A lot of people are going to need a lot of comfort. Not just tonight, but probably for several weeks. On the other hand, it's not a rule you can break for a very long time. Sooner or later, you'll see the wisdom in it, I promise!''

Will wasn't too sure what she meant by that, but he'd worry about it later. He aimed to have Ben and Sam with him tonight. And he'd like to have Jenna close by, too. He needed someone his own age to share things with.

''It's not going to be easy,'' he said.

''No,'' agreed the teacher. ''But it is going to be possible. I have faith in you, Will. And the rest of the children.''

Well, that was good. If only he had her confidence!

That night was as bad as Will had expected, but not as bad as it could have been. To his surprise, Amber had actually done a pretty decent job with the babies. She'd organized a dozen of the other kids into changing diapers, checking feed, burping, and just keeping the babies occupied. Maybe she'd found her calling. As long as she wanted to help with them, Will was glad to let her do it.

Bryan and Andrea's troops had scavenged up bedding and pillows for about thirty large beds. That meant about two and a half people to a bed, but it wasn't as bad as he'd feared. Most of the kids had younger siblings, so they could all share together without much fuss. As he'd expected, nobody wanted to be alone that first night, so there weren't any complaints about this arrangement, not even from Dave, who was still surly about not being leader.

There were plenty of tears and sniffling that night, and not just from the youngest kids, either. Ms. Pringle kept the lights going, even if it did waste power a bit. The other holoteachers seemed to have vanished now. Maybe it was to conserve power, but Will suspected it was because the computer wanted to interface with the colony now using only one face. It would be less upsetting that way, and provide some sort of stability. And they needed as much of that as they could get.

Will couldn't get to sleep, even as the crying and sniffling faded down. Sam was too young to be worried, but Ben had wanted to know where their parents were. All Will could say was: "Gone."

Ben frowned. "When will they be back?"

"They won't be coming back," Will said gently. "We're on our own now."

"Oh." Ben was struggling to understand this. "I want Mom and Dad."

"So do I," Will admitted. "But there's nothing we can do about it. We have to look after each other now."

"Okay," Ben agreed. But he'd still looked troubled, and he'd sniffled a lot until he fell asleep.

Will wondered what he was going to do. Ben and Sam were really too young to understand death yet. So were all the other youngsters. But the older ones knew the truth, and everyone was bound to miss their parents sooner or later.

He missed them a lot already. He couldn't help remembering Dad this morning—so proud of what he'd done. And Mom, moving a bit slowly because she was expecting their baby sister. And they were all dead now . . .

Tears trickled down Will's cheeks, but he refused to

make a sound. He was in charge now. He couldn't help crying in the dark, but he wasn't going to let anyone else know he was doing it. His heart ached, and he felt so desperately alone, insecure, and fragile. How could he possibly lead everybody else when he felt like this?

There was a movement next to him, and then Jenna's voice, quietly: "You awake, Will?"

"Uh-huh," he answered, wiping at his tears.

"Good." She slipped into bed next to him, fully dressed, just like him. Virtually no pajamas had survived. He wondered about other clothes, and knew that was one more thing to check on tomorrow. Jenna snuggled up to him, holding him tightly. He felt dampness on his shoulder, and realized she'd been crying even more than he had. He hugged her back.

"I miss them," Jenna whispered.

"Me, too," Will admitted. For several minutes, they just lay there. His shoulder was getting damper, and he could feel Jenna's body shaking, but she, like him, cried without a sound. He knew he was dripping tears into her hair, but he didn't really care.

Eventually, she fell asleep. There were four of them in the bed, meant for one adult, so he didn't have the room to move much. He felt himself drifting, but he was still thinking about the morning—what he had to do, what he had to get others to do . . . There was so much ahead of them and he had to keep track of it.

Come what may, they *would* survive . . .

CHAPTER 5

WILL SMILED AS he saw the dragon sniffing the air cautiously. It wasn't *really* a dragon, of course; someone had called it that seven years ago when they'd first seen one, and the name had stuck. It was about six feet long, with a bulky, muscular body on stubby legs. Its leathery head had several nasty spikes protruding from a collar just behind its ears. The dragons were very tough, but they had the best meat once they'd been killed and roasted. Over the past seven years, they'd worked out the best way to kill the beasts.

But they were very suspicious, and this one was no exception. It sniffed at the air, perhaps tracing some scent of the human beings who waited for it. Its snout wrinkled, and it glanced around. Seeing nothing, it ambled slowly forward.

At which moment, Bryan and Tiffany leaped from concealment behind it, yelling and brandishing their spears. Dressed in their tree bear furs, with feathers in their hair and with bright red streaks painted down their faces, they were quite a scary sight for the nervous dragon. It took one look at them and bolted down the pathway to what it thought was safety.

The ground gave way below it, and with a howl it fell into the concealed pit. Will and Jenna dashed forward to join Bryan and Tiffany. Jenna had an arrow ready, and when the dazed dragon looked up, she shot it cleanly through the eye. It thrashed once, and then collapsed, dead. Will jumped into the pit, watching to be certain it was dead—not that Jenna ever missed, but it was never very smart to take chances—and then tied the creeper rope around the dead monster's chest. Bryan slung the other end over a branch above, and the three at the mouth of the pit hauled the dragon up. Will clambered up after it, helping to move it to the side of the hole. Together, the four of them managed to get the dead dragon onto the stretcher they had already constructed. Will and Jenna then took a handle each, and started to drag the dragon back to the colony. Tiffany and Bryan stayed behind to remove the blood from the pit so that it could be reused later.

Once it was butchered, this dragon would last the colony a good week, with reasonable rationing. Ms. Pringle always insisted that they kill the minimal amount of the local wildlife. Ecologically sound principles, she had explained. If you killed too often, the prey would die out or move to a safer area to live.

It had been a struggle to survive these past seven years. There had been one crisis after another, and always a fresh problem to solve. Somehow, though, they had always managed to beat the challenges and the odds. Only three of the children had died in those seven years, and there had been another twelve born. One of the old rules that Will had changed was that of getting married. When the adults were in charge, nobody under sixteen could get married. He'd changed it to thirteen. Partly that was because he'd discovered that once the colonists knew the facts of life and could start experimenting with them, they would. And partly it was because he and Jenna had wanted to get married to one another since they had been five years old, and he didn't see any reason to wait that much longer.

Ms. Pringle had been a bit bothered about it, but he'd talked her around. It used to be, on Earth, that most people who were thirteen were not mature enough for lifetime commitments, and wanted to check around a lot to find the right person for them. But on Tarshish, there wasn't exactly a large number of people to check out. And everyone here matured really fast because they had to, simply to survive.

As leader, Will had taken it upon himself to perform the marriages, which always took place in front of the whole colony. Ms. Pringle had performed the ceremony for him and Jenna, though she'd objected that she wasn't empowered to do such things. Will, as was so often the case these days, had simply overruled her. She hadn't protested too much, and seemed to enjoy being called upon to perform the ceremony.

A lot of other things had changed over the seven years, too. They now had a small farm working, where Adam was laboring very hard to grow as many Earth crops as he could. They had plenty of potatoes, strawberries, and to-matoes, and the corn was doing pretty well, too. Elena had become something of a chef, and had her own staff of cooks working with her to prepare the communal meals. She'd be glad of the dragon, and would have it cut up and cooking for dinner tonight. It would make a nice change from fuzzbat stew, at any rate!

Yes, overall, things had gone pretty well for the colony. Despite the fact that he always wanted to step down as leader, Will was constantly voted back in again each year. The problem was, he knew, that he had too good a track record for solving problems. Not many people wanted to go up against him, especially now that Dave was gone.

Will scowled; that was his one great failure, and he could never go very long without thinking about it. Two years ago, Dave and six of his more fanatical followers had decided to break away from the colony. Dave had always resented not being leader, and he finally refused to accept the matter any longer. With his small group, he'd announced that he was leaving, and that was that.

Unable to think of any nonviolent way to stop the breakaway, Will had been forced to allow them to leave. It really upset him, though, that anyone would leave the colony for whatever reasons. They'd survived so long only by sticking together, and Dave's move smacked of disloyalty to the group. But there had been no way to make them stay, short of force. And that was unthinkable.

The number one rule for the colony was that nobody harmed any other member of the colony in any way. One of the youths who'd left with Dave was Byron Rogers. He'd tried to get Tiffany to consent to be his mate, but she'd refused. Byron had punched Tiffany out of anger, an unthinkable offence. Will had been forced to punish Byron by caning him in public, an example to anyone else who even thought about hurting another person. There had been no more incidents like that, but Will wasn't surprised that Byron had wanted to leave after that incident.

Not that the others really missed the seven. All of them had been malcontents, and all had failed to really pull their weight. It was just the fact that *anyone* had wanted to quit the colony that rankled Will. Jenna had been glad to see them go, and felt they were better off without the "outlaws," as everyone had taken to calling them.

Will had given them all provisions for a week, and Dave had led the four boys and two girls away. None of them had been seen since, though Paul Matthews had come across traces of someone hunting out to the north. They didn't even know if any of the seven were still alive. Will wished there was some way to tell, but he had been forced to accept the situation, though nothing could make him like it.

Back at the school, Will and Jenna turned over their kill to Elena's eager hands. Then they stopped by the nursery, where Amber let them play with their daughter for a while. Amber had turned out to be a huge surprise to Will. He'd expected her to pout and carry on like Dave, but she'd done nothing of the kind. She'd taken charge of the babies from the first day, and had proven to be an absolute wonder at it. Amber had organized everything, and performed miracles to make sure her young charges had exactly what they needed. She'd tested the milk mixes that had been developed using the sheepniks—the closest thing on this world to a mammal, since it did produce an acceptable milk. As the babies had grown, she'd taken over as Ms. Pringle's assistant with great interest. Now that there were a dozen babies back in the colony—one of them her own—she'd reverted to her earlier role as colony mother. In the nursery, she laid down all of the rules, and Will would never dream of interfering with her.

And this small domain of hers, it turned out, was exactly what she was best suited for. She'd even admitted to Will at one point that she was glad he was running the colony, and that she was restricted to just the babies. "They're easier to deal with," she confessed. "And a lot more fun." Will had been a little uneasy with her at first, but now she was one of two people he relied on absolutely.

Jenna, of course, was the other. She'd always been his best friend, and that had never changed over the years. Will felt completely at ease with her, and she was always on his side, without doubt or reserve. She'd changed in many ways over time, some of them very interesting indeed! She was the best hunter they had, and absolutely uncanny with the bow and arrow. Will was good, but Jenna could outshoot everyone in the colony. She was tough, resourceful and resilient, and his second in command. Everyone respected Jenna, and none of them more than Will did.

The unreal person he relied on absolutely was, of course, Ms. Pringle. She hadn't changed at all, naturally, since she was simply a projection. She looked exactly as she had always looked, except that she'd taken to ''wearing'' sheepnik-skin clothing like most of the girls. She obviously felt that this made her more acceptable, but Will secretly missed her old clothing style. Maybe it *had* been Earth clothing, but it had made her look good.

Her advice and her sharpness hadn't changed, either. She'd taught everyone almost everything that they knew, and she had now started getting ready to teach the babies. It looked as if she had a job for life—and in her case that was likely to be several centuries. It comforted Will to know that.

Providing, of course, they had centuries. There was always the problem of the Feeders . . .

Even after seven years, he couldn't get the memories to be less painful. And, soon, they'd be back . . .

Jenna slapped his arm, jerking him out of his thoughts. ''So,'' she asked, ''what do you want to do this afternoon? More work, or''—she grinned—''you want to goof off? It's a warm day, and I can hear the lake calling our names . . .''

It was very tempting. There wasn't anything really urgent to do, and the weather was just a shade warmer than he liked. A dip in the lake with Jenna would be fun. On the other hand, it set a bad example to everyone if he played about too much. He couldn't ask people to work if he wasn't willing to do the same.

''Later,'' he said, sighing. ''I think right now we'd better check and see how Sara's construction projects are going.'' Sara had developed an interest in architecture, and had convinced Will that it was time to start building homes for people. Being forced to work outside so much, they had all lost their former distrust of the open air. In fact, most of them never went indoors unless they had lessons scheduled. Will had agreed that building houses was called for. He liked the idea of having somewhere he and Jenna could have privacy together. At the moment, they were likely to be interrupted at any time by any colonist with a problem. In one way, that was good, because it meant that they stayed very hands-on with what was happening. At other times it could be very frustrating.

"Spoilsport," muttered Jenna, but she was still smiling. "You just don't like getting clean, that's all."

"Yes, I always hated baths," Will agreed, as they started off. "If it wasn't for you volunteering to scrub my back, I doubt I'd ever take one."

"I'll scrub it now," she offered.

"Don't tempt me," he begged her. "I really think we should do some work first."

"We *did* some work," Jenna pointed out. "Dragon hunting, remember?"

"I know," Will agreed. "It's just—" He broke off as he heard his name being called. Tom Beatty, one of the nine-year-olds, was hurrying from the schoolhouse and calling his name. What was wrong? Jenna stopped teasing him as they changed direction to meet Tom.

"Miz wants to see you," Tom said, panting. Most of the youngsters called Ms. Pringle simply "Miz." "Says it's very urgent."

Will nodded, and took off as fast as he could. Jenna fell into step with him. Ms. Pringle never asked to see him unless it really was something. The last time had been when the tree bears had cornered a hunting party. Her flying bots had alerted her, and Will had managed to lead a rescue party. That had been when they'd lost one of the colonists, though, mauled to death by a bear.

What could possibly be wrong this time? There were no hunting parties out—he'd seen Bryan and Tiffany returning. The horrible thought that constantly lurked below the surface bubbled out again: Maybe the Feeders were on their way again.

Ms. Pringle met them at the door to the schoolhouse, the farthest she could travel. "Will, Jenna, I'm glad you were so close. You'd better come inside."

"What is it, Ms. Pringle?" Will asked, catching his breath again. He was in excellent shape, so the run hadn't really winded him.

"Something I never expected to happen," she replied, leading him into the closest classroom. There was a holo-image running already, showing Tarshish from space. "Several of the satellites the older colonists seeded as they entered this solar system are still working," she explained. "As a result, I monitor them constantly, just in case." A point of light winked on close to the eighth planet. "As a result, I detected the ship immediately."

"Ship?" Will asked, confused.

"Yes," Ms. Pringle answered. "A human ship has just entered the Tarshish system. It looks as though rescue has arrived at last."

Will was stunned. Rescue? But . . . they didn't *need* to be rescued. Everyone was fine. He stared at the small light in consternation. But would the visitors believe that? After all, they were bound to be adults.

How would they respond to a civilization of children?

CHAPTER 6

"**D**O YOU HAVE any idea how bored I am?" asked First Lieutenant Robert Mason, leaning back in his seat, hands clasped behind his head, staring at the ceiling.

"Almost as bored as I am of hearing you say that?" Nicola Moore guessed. She resisted the temptation to copy his pose, and glanced at the *Wanderer*'s status. It was, as it always was, fine. But Moore took her responsibility as captain very seriously. Maybe *too* seriously, which was probably why she was still captaining a scout ship instead of a nice, cushy job on a cruise liner somewhere. Her reputation was that of a no-nonsense hardliner. In short, she was hard as nails and cold as ice. Then again, the thought of having to deal with cruise passengers complaining about their food, or that the stars were kind of dull to look out at after several days didn't appeal to her at all.

Exploring the unknown, however, did. Except for the long pauses when there was nothing to explore, such as right now. Mason wasn't the only bored one; the entire crew was getting the jitters. This flight had been longer than normal, and they were still several months out from their target. Moore could almost feel the sand between her toes, and the warm sun of some vacation spot on her back. The last three systems they'd explored had all been totally inhospitable. Gas giants and bleak, cold, sterile planets. Not exactly thrilling to explore, and totally without prospects for colonists.

And now they were passing through this system, which had been explored two decades ago. Moore ran her eye across the data as a matter of habit. One inhabitable world, named Tarshish, colonized almost a decade ago. She wondered idly if it would be worthwhile stopping there for a quick break. It would slow their return to Earth, but it would give them a chance to stretch their legs a bit and see some fresh faces. To be honest, after five years out with this crew, she *needed* to see some fresh faces.

However, she'd been on colony worlds before. They were generally focused on their own survival and didn't appreciate visitors. And they hardly ever had any luxuries anyway. They'd be resented if they stopped off, so Moore decided to give it a pass. It might have been nice, but it would more likely be irritating.

She and Mason were the only crew on the flight deck right now. Unless there were problems or surveys to run, they were more than enough to keep the ship humming, plus Valdez down in the engine room, of course. The other nine crew members were off duty, doing whatever they could to stave off their own boredom. Nicola Moore almost envied them, except she found her own downtime to be mostly wasted. They were all getting stagnant, and all looking forward to the return to Earth.

This meant that they were all slipping a bit in basic safety, which could be lethal in space. She wondered about organizing another fake emergency to test their reflexes. On the other hand, the last two had served more to irritate people than to keep them on their toes. Another test would most likely get them grumbling. As it was, Ensign Akiko Tsu and Crewman Alan Warren were hardly speaking to her. Not that she really *cared,* of course, but the thought of alienating any more of the crew wasn't exactly appealing. She knew that the captain traditionally was a loner, but there wasn't any point in pushing things to the extreme where none of them would speak to her.

Nicola Moore knew that the crew were all inventing whatever they could to keep boredom at arms length. Some of it, no doubt, was against regulations—like the card game that Mason ran in his cabin. But as long as she didn't officially know about these things, she figured it was best to let them have their diversions, as long as they didn't harm the ship. Grief, she could do with a few more diversions of her own, she had to admit. It was just a shame that, as captain, she had to stay aloof from the rest of the crew for the sake of discipline. That meant no romantic attachments, for one thing. The last thing she needed was for anyone to think she was giving preferential treatment to a lover; that kind of thing could destroy crew morale faster than almost anything. Staying celibate for five years had been rough, but not as rough as the alternatives. Besides, to be frank, there wasn't any one of the crew that she would have liked to spend any more time with than she had to—and definitely none of them she'd like to wake up next to in the morning.

"Status?" she asked Mason.

He yawned, and then cocked an eye at his panel. "Fine," he drawled. "Just like it always is." He didn't take his feet off the console. "You want to play I Spy?"

"No," Moore answered.

"How about Ghost, then?"

"We're on duty," Nicola Moore pointed out. "We're supposed to be alert and ready for anything."

"I *am* ready for anything," he objected. "But it just never happens."

"How about you cuttin' the chatter," she said.

"Yes, sir!" muttered Mason sarcastically.

Nicola sighed. Another four hours to go before the end of this shift. Another mind-numbing four hours with Mason. She considered changing him to another shift, but who would she put in his place that would be any better? Five years was way too long to coop a dozen people up together and expect them to remain interesting to one another. In fact—

The ship shook suddenly, and half the board lit up with red lights. A whooping sound filled the flight deck with an ear-splitting noise. Mason fell off his chair, and then scrambled to his feet as the deck buckled and heaved.

Moore dived for the panel, trying to make some sort of sense out of what was going on. It was an emergency of some kind, but what? "Shut off that bloody siren!" she yelled, unable to hear herself think. Mason seemed to have the same thing in mind, because the noise died almost instantly.

According to her panel, there had been some sort of disruption down in engineering. She was showing pressure loss, a hull breach . . . God, what was going on down there? She tried the internal scanner, without success. Then she switched to the external view, looking aft.

"What's going on?" Mason demanded, his voice filled with worry. "This isn't making any sense."

"I'm trying to find out," she snapped. The picture came up and she couldn't stifle a shocked gasp.

There was a large hole in the outer hull, venting air and debris into space. It appeared to be somewhere in the region of the engine room.

"God," she whispered, and then checked that the emergency bulkheads had sealed around the area. They had, but it meant that the engine room was completely inaccessible for the moment. "Try and get through to Valdez," she ordered Mason. Meanwhile, she started to check on the power flow reports. Engineering had been damaged, that much was clear. How, she didn't have a clue as yet. The power levels were dropping, and she considered shutting down the thrust completely, in case of problems. That could be done from up here. There was always the chance that it might explode if left running in this emergency situation. On the other hand, there was also the possibility that if she did shut it down, they might not be able to start it up again. She scanned the readings with concern, and decided that as long as they didn't show anything out of the norm, she'd leave things alone.

"No reply," Mason reported. "I think the comm panel down there has been damaged."

The door to the flight deck opened, and Tsu came in, her face creased with worry. "What's happening?"

"I don't know yet," Moore replied. "Some sort of explosion in the engine room's caused a hull breach. Tsu, you and"—she glanced over the Asian woman's shoulder and saw Warren arriving—"Warren get suited up. I'm going to need someone to go in there."

"Right." They both turned and hurried away. Well, at least they couldn't complain about being bored any longer!

What had happened wasn't quite as important right now as what *would* happen. If the drive showed any signs of fluctuating, it could go critical and destroy the ship. She had to stay on top of that. "Mason, send a drone out to check the breach," she ordered. She had a diagnostic running, measuring the power levels and projecting possible consequences. Then she checked the air levels. "Damn. The air plant seems to have suffered damage, too." They'd lost a quarter of their air in the explosion, before the shutters had locked down. And the instruments showed that no more was being generated. That could become a real problem very shortly. But that was hours off, so she could afford to ignore it for the moment. She needed to know precisely what else had been affected, and how.

"Drone launched," Mason reported. He was guiding it from his panel by remote. Nicola Moore spared a second to glance at the screen, seeing what the drone could see. At the moment, it was crawling down the skin of the ship, heading for the breach. She turned back to the console to check on her diagnostic progress. Her heart was still racing, and she was breathing quickly and shallowly.

Some of the food circuits were out, too, and the water purification. That was right next to the engine room, so it was only to be expected. Again, that would be a serious problem, but not immediately, so she filed it away for future worry. Right now, her main concern was power.

The diagnostic finished running, and the bad news came thick and fast. The main generator was damaged, and would have to be shut down. It had begun to overheat already. The secondary was damaged, too, but to a lesser degree. It could be kept working, but at a reduced work load. At least the third generator, the one that supplied the ship's circuits with power, was undamaged. They wouldn't lose life support, or power to the controls. On the other hand, without the main generator, they couldn't get back to Earth. Faced with no option, she started the shut-down process.

"Drone's going in," Mason reported. Moore nodded, and looked up from her work to check out what it was seeing.

The picture showed the drone entering the damaged hull section. It had to be at least six or eight feet across. The air had stopped venting, since it was all gone. At least the debris had been blown clear of the ship, too, so there was nothing sharp hanging about to cause problems. The lighting was out inside the engine room, so Mason switched on the drone's spotlights.

Captain Moore whistled at the scene. The main generator was visible, with a chunk missing from its side. No wonder it wasn't running properly! Half the safeties must have been blown apart! The secondary generator had some odd damage and staining. Moore realized what it was and almost threw up. It had to be parts of Valdez's body that had been driven into the controls by the force of the explosion. Mason moved the camera quickly, clearly as bothered by the sight as Nicola was. Well, now they knew why there was no reply from the engineer . . .

"What the hell is *that*?" she demanded, staring at shattered wreckage that came into view beside the main generator. It was twisted and buckled, and like nothing that was supposed to be in the room at all. She realized that this had to be what had exploded, since all of it had shattered outward.

Mason looked uncomfortable, and Moore realized that he knew. "What?" she demanded in her don't-mess-with-me voice.

"Valdez's still," Mason said quietly.

"His *what*?" Nicola growled, even though she was starting to get the picture.

"His still," Mason repeated, squirming. "We ran out of alcohol a couple of months back, you see, and he was . . ."

"Making his own," Nicola Moore finished grimly. "And supplying the rest of you with some, too, no doubt, so you'd not mention this to me." She held in her anger; there wasn't much point in getting mad with Valdez. He'd paid the price for his stupidity. But she had no intention of letting Mason or anyone else who knew about this get off lightly. "Well, *now* I think you can see why that's against regulations." She scowled at the picture. "And the damned thing exploded and has damaged my ship. We'll talk about this later," she promised. Turning to the comm unit, she tapped the button. "Tsu? Warren? You ready to go yet?"

"Almost," Tsu replied. "Two minutes."

"Move it," Nicola ordered. "There's a six foot or so gap in the outer hull, but nothing floating in there that could damage you. You're going to have to seal the breach as soon as possible. Then check out the air plant. It seems to be off-line.''

"Understood.''

"Where the hell is everybody else?'' complained Moore.

"Down here,'' Tsu answered. "Everyone's getting ready to help.''

"Well, *don't*,'' Moore ordered. "I want just Tsu and Warren in there right now.''

"Captain,'' Anneke Larson complained, "more of us in there would get the place sealed faster.''

"And you'd get in each other's way,'' the captain pointed out. "Besides, endangering two of you is enough for my conscience right now. If Tsu gives the all clear, the rest of you can go in. Not until, understand?''

"Yes, Captain,'' Larson agreed. Nicola Moore could hear the reluctance in the other woman's voice.

"Well,'' she said, looking over at Mason, "I guess this means nobody's bored anymore.''

Two hours later, the patch was in place, and the sealed section had been repressurized. The rest of the crew had been able to get into the damaged section, Nicola Moore with them. It was not good. After a brief examination, she called a staff meeting on the flight deck. It was cramped there, but she had Larson and Mason watching the controls and running further diagnostics while she explained their situation.

"The main generator's out,'' Moore pointed out. "The coils have been twisted, and need to be straightened. A two-hour job in a shop—if we had one around. Until then, we're out of super-c. That means no return to Earth until repairs are made. *If* we can make them.

"Generator two's on reduced power, but there's sufficient power to keep us flying. The power generator's fine, so that's one thing we don't have to worry about. However, life support's been shot to hell. Part of the explosion from the still knocked out the adjoining wall, crushing several key sections of the recycling system. That means no fresh water and no fresh air. Panjit?''

Vikram Panjit, the chief medical officer, cleared his throat nervously. ''The air will last us two days or so before it gets unbreathable,'' he replied. ''Water recirculation is effectively dead. All we have is whatever's in the system now. Used for drinking only, a maximum of one day. And the food processors' short, so this is a real good time for us all to start those diets we've been putting off.''

''In short,'' she summed up, ''thanks to the fact that Mason and some others of you covered up the existence of Valdez's stupid operation, we're in a very grave situation. Accent here on *grave*. I'll kick the relevant backsides later. Valdez is lucky he died, I promise you that much. It's better than he'd have gotten from me.'' She studied their faces, some ashamed, all scared sick.

''There's one piece of good news in all of this,'' she said finally. She gestured at the screens. ''We're within a day's flight, even on reduced power, of a habitable planet. Better, one that was seeded with a human colony some years ago. It's probably not got much high-tech left, but it's possible that they'll have *something* we may be able to salvage for the ship. And, with luck, we can strip the damaged sections of the generators and recycling plant and fix them.''

''I'm not so sure about that, Captain,'' Tsu broke in, unusually formal. She'd certainly known about the still and said nothing, so she must be suffering from a guilty conscience. ''The explosion also took out some of the computer mainframe.''

Uh-oh . . . ''But everything's working fine,'' Nicola objected, gesturing around the room.

''Here, yes,'' Tsu agreed. She was the computer expert. ''The part that was ruined was the one with the engineering specs in them. The information may still be there, but it's not accessible. Even if we could repair the generator, we don't know *how* now. Unless we can get at the information, we don't have a snowball in hell's chance of mending the engines.'' She sighed. ''We may end up applying for citizenship on whatever that planet down there is called.''

Nicola Moore could feel the shock from the others almost as much as her own. She was a spacer, first and foremost, like the rest of them. The idea of being stranded on one planet for the rest of her life was the equivalent of a life sentence in jail. To be trapped like that would be unendurable . . .

CHAPTER 7

WILL KNEW HE had no choice but to call a general meeting and explain the crisis to everyone in the colony. Only those taking care of the babies were excused; they'd get the news later. Most of the ones who heard sat there in the school room, stunned.

"According to Ms. Pringle," Will concluded, "it's a small ship. It can't be bringing more colonists, unless they've come up with something radically new in the past ten years or so that she obviously wouldn't know about. Her best guess is that's it's a scout."

"But why would a scout come here?" asked Tiffany, puzzled. "This planet's already been explored."

"Exactly," Will answered. "So it's not to scout us out. Why they're coming, who can say? But what they'll do when they get here . . . Well, that's another matter entirely. Ms. Pringle?"

The teacher nodded. "The ship will be crewed by between ten and twenty people," she explained carefully, knowing she was addressing an audience who'd never seen a scout ship in their lives. "They will all be adults, of course. And when they reach here and discover that there are no adults in charge, they are almost certainly going to try and take charge."

"Take charge?" Adam yelled. "But . . . why would they do that?" Several others echoed his question.

"Because adults don't think that kids can do things right," Will said bluntly. "Those of you who can remember back to when our parents were alive will know that. Nobody under eighteen was considered smart enough to have any say in anything. They couldn't vote, they couldn't marry, and they certainly couldn't be in charge of anything." He paused and looked carefully around the room. "And we're *all* under eighteen."

That didn't take very long to sink in; nobody here was so stupid that they couldn't work out what that meant.

"They'll want to take over?" Andrea asked, confused and with an edge of irritation in her voice. "*Our* colony? They'd think we couldn't run it ourselves?"

"Most likely," Ms. Pringle agreed. "Adults tend to be very . . . concerned about youngsters. And they would undoubtedly see you as such, not as the capable people you have become."

"But . . . *how* could they do it?" asked Elena. "There's only, maybe, twenty of them. There's four times as many of us. We just wouldn't listen to them."

Will had been dreading that question. "They have weapons that we don't," he said sadly. "Don't you remember guns and lasers? Our parents had them, and these people—whose job is to chance danger—will certainly have them, and probably more. Ms. Pringle has a whole file on the sorts of weapons adults have built for themselves."

"They'd *force* us to obey them?" asked Don, incredulously.

"They'd think it was for your own good," Ms. Pringle

explained. "They'd do it only for the best of reasons. But they'd do it."

"We can't let them," Patti Baker said firmly. "This is *our* colony. They have no right to interfere."

"They don't need a *right*," Will pointed out. "If they have guns and so on, they have the *might*."

"There's got to be something we can do," Tiffany insisted.

"There is," Will agreed. "But, first, there's another point we should consider." He looked at Jenna and she nodded.

"This is a scout ship," Jenna informed them all. "It won't stay here. Oh, it might leave some of its crew behind, but they won't *all* stay. It'll be going on, probably back to Earth. Since those ships can carry a couple of dozen people, it means that if anyone wants to leave, they might be able to go back to Earth on the ship."

That was met by a stunned silence. It was something none of them had considered, that was obvious. Will wished it hadn't occurred to him, either. But it had to be mentioned and faced. "Nobody's saying anyone *should* go," he said carefully. "Just that it's possible if anyone *wants* to go."

Tiffany shook her head. "Why would anyone want to go?" she asked. "*This* is our home. We've fought for it, and worked for it. If we went back to Earth, we'd be considered children, wouldn't we?"

"Yes," agreed Ms. Pringle.

"Then I don't want to go," Tiffany decided. She looked around the room. "Why would anyone want to go?" she repeated.

"Because they have a lot of things on Earth that we don't have here," Will answered honestly. "You've all been taught by Ms. Pringle. You've seen the sort of things that they have back there. Technology. Science. A lot of things we don't have, and will never have."

Adam snorted. "Right. But they don't have what's most important. They don't have *us*. We're a colony, Will. I wouldn't want to leave anybody here. Not even Amber, even if she can be a pain in the butt." That got a round of laughter, and Amber pretended to be annoyed. "I don't want to leave this, to go to a bunch of strangers."

Will was pleased with their answers, but he knew it wasn't that simple. They were reacting, not thinking things through. He glanced at Ms. Pringle, wanting her to state the hard part. She understood, and nodded slightly.

"You may not have an option," the teacher said gently. "They have guns, remember? And they think that they know better than you what's good for you. They may decide that they will take some of you back with them, purely for your own good."

"No!" Adam exclaimed. "They couldn't be that bad! Could they?"

"We don't know until they arrive," Will answered. "They might be better, but they might be worse. The thing that we have to bear in mind constantly is that they're *adults*. They'll think we don't know enough to be on our own, or be in charge. They'll assume they know best, and ignore whatever we say or want, simply because they're older than us."

That silenced everyone again. Will could see that they were all thinking about what he had just said, and reaching pretty much the same conclusions that he had. Eventually, Amber asked: "Then what can we do about it?"

"We have to avoid them," Will said. "We can't let them know there are no adults here. We have to stay out of their way, and let them know they're not wanted. Then, maybe, they'll go away."

"*Maybe*?" echoed Adam. He shook his head. "Will, with all due respect, that's just not good enough. We need better than *maybe*."

"I'm open to any and all suggestions," Will said simply.

"I don't think that your opinions aren't worth listening to. I'm not an adult—yet." That got a chuckle or two, at least.

"I say we *make* them go away," Adam stated. "We meet them, and stop them from coming out here. Make them go away again."

"How?" asked Jenna, shaking her head. "Lasers against arrows? No contest, Adam. We'd lose, fast."

"Only if they saw us," Adam insisted. "We could get just one or two of them, as a warning. Then they'd get the message and go."

"No, they wouldn't," Jenna replied. "If we got one of them, they'd come after us."

"Wait a minute!" Will said, shocked. "Time out, here. Adam, are you talking about *injuring* them?"

"Injuring," he agreed casually. "Or killing, if necessary."

Will was stunned. He looked at his friend as if he'd only just seen him for the first time. "Adam, our primary rule is that we *never* hurt one another."

"I know," Adam said. "And it's the best possible rule. But *they're* not us. They don't obey our rules. So our rules don't apply to them."

There was some muttering about this, both for and against. Will didn't like it, and immediately said so. "We can't bend the rule," he said firmly. "Maybe they're *not* of us. But they're human. I think the rule should apply to them, whether they approve of it or not. I *really* think it would be a very bad thing to hurt one of them, let alone kill them."

"It's the best thing," Adam insisted.

"It would be suicide," Jenna countered. "Their weapons are much stronger than ours. And they'll have all sorts of technology, too, that we couldn't fight. I think Will's right, and we should just avoid them."

"You think Will's right?" Elena echoed. "Wow,

where's the surprise in that? You *always* think Will's right. And usually he is. But is he right about this?''

"To be honest,'' Will said, ''I don't know. That's why I called this meeting. I wanted you all to know what was happening, what could happen, and to help me figure out what we should do about it. I want to hear what everyone thinks, because we've only got a couple of hours before the scout ship lands, and we have to have our plans well underway by then, whatever we decide to do.''

"It may not have been the smartest idea to admit that you're unsure,'' Jenna muttered to him, as everyone in the room started talking and arguing with their neighbors.

"Maybe not,'' Will agreed, realizing she had a point. "But I won't lie to everybody, Jenna. *Maybe* I am wrong.''

"You're not wrong, Will,'' Ms. Pringle said. ''Avoidance of the problem is your best solution to this mess. If the scouts don't see anyone, they'll assume that there are adults here. They'll wonder why everyone's hiding, of course, but they'll most likely think it's just some strange cultural thing. If they see you and realize that there aren't any adults, though, they're *bound* to interfere. It's in their nature.''

"What about Adam's suggestion about fighting them?'' Will asked. ''Maybe I'm the wrong person to judge it, because I'm so opposed to any kind of fighting. Could he be right?''

"No,'' Ms. Pringle answered. ''Jenna's right—it would be suicidal. If you were to injure or kill one of the crew, the others would feel that they had to retaliate in order to punish you, and to prevent further injuries or deaths to their members. Undoubtedly some of the colonists would be hurt or even killed in return. Violence only leads to further violence.''

Will looked out over the room. Everybody was still discussing their feelings with anyone who'd listen. ''Well, let's hope we can convince them all that we're right,'' he said. He didn't know whether they'd listen or not. After a few more minutes, he had Ms. Pringle clear her throat really loudly as a signal for them all to shut up and pay attention.

"Right," he said, looking at their worried faces. "You've all heard what suggestions have been made, and you've had a chance to think and talk about it. My idea is that we simply stay away from the scout ship, and hide out until it goes away. Adam's suggestion is that we attack them when they land and injure or kill one or more of them in order to convince them to go away. Now, I think that's dangerous for two reasons. One, they'd only fight back, and two . . . it would get us into a bad habit. If we injure one of them today . . . will we injure one of *us* tomorrow? I know Adam thinks my plan of hiding isn't enough, and maybe he's right. Maybe the scouts will come after us. If they do, *then* we can try and think of something else. Now, think about which of these options would work best. And then we'll vote on it."

Adam nodded. "And if I win, will you go along with it?"

"Not exactly," Will admitted. "If you all decide to attack, I won't help. I think it's wrong to hurt *anyone,* even if they're not one of us. And I won't do it. But I won't stop you if that's what the majority decides."

"Fair enough," Adam agreed. "Well, then—a vote! Who's with me, and who's with Will?" He moved to stand several feet away from Will.

Amber immediately moved to join Will, head high and serious. "I look after the helpless," she said. "I won't hurt anyone, either."

The rest of the colonists started to move, some quickly, some more slowly as they weighed up their choices. It became apparent very quickly, though, that most sided with Will. Only six people joined Adam.

"Right," Will said. "We've decided." He looked at Adam. "Are you with us?"

After a moment, Adam nodded. "I still think you're wrong," he admitted. "But if the colony agrees with you, I'll go along with that." He and his six moved back to join the rest.

Will was pleased that there were no hard feelings about this. The vote could have split Adam off, but he was glad that Adam understood that the group as a whole had to be supported.

"Right, we have to plan quickly," Will said. "Amber, can the babies be moved without a problem? We'll have to take them into the woods for at least a couple of days, I'd say."

"They're all in good shape," Amber answered. "And we can bring along enough supplies. The only one I'm worried about is Patti."

Will glanced at his friend. She was eight months pregnant now, and quite large. "Will you be able to keep up with us?" he asked her kindly.

"Will you be able to keep up with me?" she asked, jutting her chin out. "I can march rings around you all."

Laughing, Will nodded. "I guess you could at that. Okay, we have to bring along what we can."

"What about Ms. Pringle?" asked Tiffany, worried. "We can't bring her along. And the scouts are bound to find her."

"I don't think they'll damage me," the teacher replied. "And they can't control me, or force me to tell them anything about you. My programming will not allow it."

"They might damage you," Adam said bluntly. "Or reprogram you."

"They may *try*," Ms. Pringle said. "But I am programmed to defend myself."

"How?" asked Adam. "Karate?" That got a worried laugh.

"I can generate electrical charges," Ms. Pringle informed them. "From unpleasant to lethal, depending upon need. Anyone attempting injury to me would suffer injury first, I assure you. But I would not act without provocation," she added for Will's benefit.

"Then I guess we can be as ready as we have to be very shortly," Will decided. "Everything else is suspended for now. Until this scout ship is gone, we hide. Everyone get what they need, and we'll meet outside here in half an hour."

Everyone began moving. Jenna and Will stayed with Ms. Pringle. Adam lingered, and then said: "There's one more thing to consider. I didn't want to mention it in front of everyone, Will. I think you're wrong, but I respect you. But Dave won't. What will *he* do when the scout ship lands? He's bound to spot it."

Will had been hoping nobody would ask that question because he didn't have an answer for it. There was simply no telling what Dave would do.

He could only hope that it would be nothing foolish enough to get the whole colony into trouble. However, given Dave's nature, he couldn't be too optimistic on that score. Nobody in the colony would go against Will's plan. But he could virtually guarantee that Dave would . . .

CHAPTER 8

CAPTAIN NICOLA MOORE. Once she'd dreamed of being in this position. Now, however, it was more like a nightmare. The *Wanderer* was damaged and limping along. She supposed they were lucky not to have been blown up by Valdez's stupidity— compounded by God knew how many of the crew turning a blind eye to his illicit still—but she couldn't bring herself to feel it. The prospect of being stranded on the planet below was too grim. She'd almost sooner have been dead.

"Any radio contact?" she asked Mason. He was being unusually docile right now, no doubt because of his own guilt in this business. He was probably afraid she'd make him get out and walk the rest of the way home. If they didn't need every hand aboard for the repairs, it would have been a very tempting idea.

"Not a squeak," he replied, checking his instruments again. "I've scanned the planet, and there's just one colony. But there's no energy signature, and no sign of any communications net."

Moore frowned. "No energy signature? How can that be? Surely they must be using *some* form of energy down there?"

"It's possible that it's all passive," Tsu offered from her post. "Solar collectors, that kind of thing. We'd never be able to detect it."

"And no comm net?" asked Mason. "Even if they're not using atomic power or some other generators, they *have* to need a comm net."

Tsu shrugged. "Maybe they're back-to-nature boys?" she suggested. "Some colonists have very strange ideas."

"Like enjoying living on planets," agreed Moore. "Still, there are other possibilities, though I don't like to think about them."

"Like they're all dead, you mean?" Mason deduced. "Frankly, I think we have to consider the possibility. Seven colonies I've heard about have died out so far, for one reason or another." He gestured at the globe on the screen. "This could be number eight."

Moore winced at the thought. "I hope not," she said. "We could really use their help. Any signs of where they might be?"

"I'm getting some information," he answered, checking his screens. "I've detected a couple of satellites . . . Still functional, too. They must have scanned our approach."

"So whoever's down there should know we're on our way in," mused Moore. "They *should* be trying to talk to us."

"If they're still there," Mason countered.

"And *if* they want to talk," Tsu added. "If they're a fanatical cult or something, they might not want us down there."

Moore hadn't considered that. Years before a number of colonies had been established as "religious retreats." One she remembered was founded by a group of radical environmentalists, another by a militant branch of the *American Firsters*. Neither had been receptive to outsiders. If Tarshish was like that, they were in real trouble. "Great," she muttered. Then she chuckled. "Tarshish is a Biblical name, right? Maybe we've got a planetful of nuns below us."

"Hail President Sally Field!" joked Tsu, referring to the smarmy television character, *The Flying Nun*.

"Maybe they'll be tired of their vows of chastity," Mason said with a leering grin.

"Ever hopeful," Tsu muttered, rolling her eyes. "They *might* be monks, you know."

"They might be *anything*," Nicola Moore said, before the conversation deteriorated further. "Let's not play games yet. What about a landing site?"

"I'm picking up a cultivated section near the coast of one continent," Mason answered. "Scans indicate buildings, but not much metal."

"Well, that means they at least made it down safely," Moore said. "That's a good sign. They must have picked the colony ships apart for construction, but maybe there's enough left for us to scavenge something we can use."

"Why not wish for Santa Claus to greet us with a new mainframe, too?" asked Mason.

Nicola realized she was probably being too hopeful. But, dammit, she needed *something* to hope for, and so far this planet was giving them zip. "Plot a course to land us as close to the colony as possible," she ordered Tsu, ignoring Mason's jibe. "But preferably not into a corn field. We don't want to annoy any farmers."

"Understood," Tsu agreed, bending to her task.

Turning back to the viewscreen, Nicola Moore watched the image of Tarshish growing larger. She rubbed her temples, trying to stave off the headache she could feel growing. She couldn't shake off a feeling that this wasn't going to be easy. Then again, with a broken generator, the mainframe isolated, and a hole in the hull, how *could* it be easy? Even if, as Mason had joked, Santa was down there with gifts for them all.

This was going to be trouble, she could tell. It might not be logical to rely on her hunches like this, but Nicola knew better than to ignore them. They'd saved her life more than once.

"Got it," Tsu said. "Course laid in, and ready for burn." She glanced up, apologetically. "It's going to be rough. Some of the controls are fed from the mainframe, so I'm having to bypass them."

"Hey, I always liked a roller coaster myself," Mason replied with a grin.

"Yeah," Moore said sourly. "Maybe we can have all the fun of the fair." She slapped the inboard communicator. "Captain to all hands. We're going in for a landing, and I've been warned it's going to be rough. If there's anything breakable that hasn't already broken, strap it in. Then follow suit. We're firing in five minutes." She switched off and nodded at Tsu. "Do your best, Akiko," she said softly.

"Definitely," Tsu promised, with a slight smile. It wasn't often that Nicola Moore called any of them by their first name. She generally liked to keep her distance.

Five minutes later, the *Wanderer* shook as the retros kicked into action. The planet filled the screen now, and Moore could make out the landing area without any problem. Even from orbit, she could see it. Most of the continent was a chain of mountains, and the rest was jungle. Only one area had been cleared for cultivation. It never ceased to amaze her that Mankind could alter a planet so much that you could see the results from space. Even on a backwater planet like this.

The shaking got worse, and she was forced to don her own seat restraints, for the first time ever. Obviously the jets were firing slightly out of synch, with the obvious result. Well, some people paid money for a ride like this . . .

"Entering planetary atmosphere," Mason called. He had to be very careful which buttons he aimed for. With all the shaking, his hand could be thrown off course as he stabbed at them. Moore was keeping her own hands off her controls. She was clutching her armrests, trying to stay in her seat.

Shuddering and groaning, the *Wanderer* plunged into the rarified air on the edge of Tarshish's atmosphere. Heat blazed ahead of them from the friction of their passage. The buffeting immediately became worse.

"Damn," Mason said. "It's going to be scrambled eggs for breakfast from now on."

"How can you even think about food?" asked Tsu. She looked as though she were going through the pangs of motion sickness, tossed back and forth in her seat.

Moore's stomach agreed with that assessment. She felt sick herself. The ship shuddered continually as it plunged. "How's the patch holding up?" she called.

"Frying a little at the edges," Mason answered. "But it's keeping its integrity. It should hold for the landing. I just hope that *we* do. I think my bones are turning into mush."

"They'll match your brains, then," Moore informed him. She watched their target area growing larger. "How much longer do we have to suffer this, Tsu?"

"Ten minutes, max," Tsu promised. "We've got to shed some heat, I'm afraid. I've targeted us at the edge of the jungle, and I don't think we'd make a good impression if we set everything on fire."

Nicola Moore nodded. It was good thinking, typical of Tsu. It was just a shame that it lengthened their descent . . .

But finally it was over. They were skimming the trees, and the retros had been cut. They were simply gliding in for a landing now, and that stabilized the ship. They were moving too fast for her to get a good look at what the native trees were like, but they appeared tall and green, pretty much like back on Earth. Chlorophyll in their leaves, then. A compatible ecology to humans, possibly. The colonists might be able to eat the plants here, and maybe some of the animals.

They might even have *real* steaks . . . After all this time in space, the only thing Moore missed about planets was their food. Eating restructured protein, no matter how well it was done, was never really a fulfilling meal. Still, at least it meant that nobody ever gained weight on space trips. Nobody was ever tempted to ask for a second helping of anything. To be able to eat real food again . . . *That* was almost worth blowing a hole in her ship.

Tsu started to brake the *Wanderer* for their landing, her touch on the controls gentle and precise. It felt so good not to be shaking anymore, but she kept her restraints on. It never hurt to play it safe in any planetary landing.

Tsu's fingers danced across the controls, and Nicola felt the ship shudder as the landing jets flashed. Their airspeed died almost entirely, and they were falling gently toward the trees ahead. Then the trees flashed below the ship, and she saw a cleared area, with some sort of grain crop growing. The *Wanderer* shuddered for the last time, and then dropped vertically down to the ground. A second later, the main drive shut down. The background hum that they'd been hearing for months ceased, and near-silence descended.

"A lovely landing, Akiko," Captain Moore complimented.

"Thank you." Tsu was scanning the area. "Hmmm . . . That's funny. No signs of human life," she reported. "Somebody must have known we were coming."

"Maybe they're shy?" suggested Moore. "Or worried. The ship's still a little hot."

"Maybe they're dead," Mason said bluntly, giving voice to Moore's own worst fears.

"No," Tsu contradicted. She pointed at the growing

grain. ''That's fresh this year, and if you look closely, you can see that it's been weeded recently. There are people alive here.''

For the first time in quite a few hours, Nicola Moore felt a slight surge of hope. However . . . ''If they're alive,'' she muttered, ''then where are they? Why aren't they here?'' She shook her head. ''I have a feeling this isn't going to be as simple as it should be.''

''What ever is?'' asked Tsu with a sigh.

True . . . Nicola Moore stared at the screen. Where was everybody?

CHAPTER 9

"THIS SITUATION HAS interesting possibilities," murmured Dave. He grinned at Byron, and then at another boy, a newcomer to the group. Don McGregor. The kid was a runt, and had a pimply face and mean, rodent-like little eyes. Behind the kid's back Dave even called him *Rat*. It was a name that suited him. "It looks like I was right to have you stay with Brandis and his wimps. It's always good to have a secret agent."

The boy puffed out his tiny chest, pleased with the compliment. "I knew you'd want to hear this news, sir," he said, glowing with his own self-importance.

Dave nodded absently. The truth was he couldn't have cared less about what the kid thought. The only reason Dave hadn't allowed Rat to accompany him when he'd led the splinter group was that he couldn't stand him. The kid was a jerk. But, as he'd just proven, a useful jerk. It didn't hurt to make the idiot think he was a lot more valuable than he really was. "And I'm very pleased with this information you've brought us," Dave told him. "Now, you'd better go back and keep your eyes and ears open. We'll need to know if the situation changes at all. You're doing a terrific job."

Rat beamed with pride, nodded, and then hurried away. Turning to Byron, Dave said softly: "Fetch the rest." Byron nodded, and hurried off. Dave stared at the sky, thoughtfully, and stroked his thin beard. He'd been trying for a long time to think of some way to get his revenge on Will Brandis and show the rest that he, and not that fool, should be their leader. This was the perfect opportunity, if he played it right . . .

Living and surviving in the forests was tougher than being part of the colony, but at least he didn't have to deal with all the distractions of the colony. Off-colony there was no question who ruled: Dave. The problem was that there were only seven of them in the tribe. It wasn't large enough to be viable in the long term. He had to rejoin the main group—but on his terms, not theirs. Besides, there were only two girls with him, and that had led to arguments among the other four boys. Crystal Bertram was his, and nobody dared argue with that, but that left only Donna Hanover for the other four to fight over. Dave was worried their endless squabbling could lead to a breakup of the tribe. And then where would he be? The tribe needed more girls, but none of the Brandis colonists wanted to join them.

He'd toyed with the idea of leading an attack on the colony to kidnap some members, but that would lead to more trouble, he knew. Brandis wouldn't just let him waltz into the colony and take who he wanted; it would undermine his leadership. So he'd be forced to retaliate. And with all of the colonists on his side, plus that computer, Dave knew he wouldn't stand a chance. The only workable solution was to discredit Brandis somehow, so that Dave could return as a hero and take over leadership of the colony, as he should have done from the start.

Byron returned with the others in tow, and Dave grinned at them all. "The time has come," he said softly, "for us to act. We've been given the perfect opportunity to take over the colony. There's a ship coming in."

"A ship?" Crystal perked up at the news. "Why's it here?"

"Who knows?" Dave asked. "That's not important. What *is* important is that Brandis has decided that the colony should have nothing to do with the off-worlders. There was some debate about fighting them, but, as usual, Brandis opted for the chicken way out, and he's ordered everybody to simply hide away from the ship."

Donna scowled. "Will that work?" she asked. "Surely the people in the ship must know we're here. They're bound to look for us."

"It doesn't matter whether his plan will work or not," Dave snapped. "Because I'm—*we're*—not going to give it a chance. We're going to make certain that the off-worlders go after the colony, and especially after Brandis."

Byron frowned. "I don't get it," he admitted. "Why should we even care? Isn't this ship a chance to get off this stinking planet and back to somewhere civilized?"

"And what? Go back to Earth? To be ruled by adults?" Dave gave him a filthy look. "This is *my* planet," he answered. "I'm not going anywhere. I'm going to rule it. If you want to flee, that's your business. But until you do, you'll do what I say when I say."

Crystal sighed. "And what's your great plan?" she asked. "What are your puny weapons compared to the colony's?"

Dave shot her a reproving glance. He didn't like her attitude at all. Lately she had, on several occasions, seemed to challenge his authority. If she wasn't so good-looking, he'd have thrown her out a long time ago. Once he was in charge of the colony, though, he'd have his pick of the girls. And that was when Crystal would get a boot firmly planted on her rear end. But, for now, he had to pretend that she didn't irritate him so much. "We make sure what Brandis didn't want to happen happens," he explained. "We start a fight with the off-worlders, and make sure he gets the blame for it."

There was a moment of silence, and then Crystal asked: "And how, exactly, do we do that?"

"By using my brains," he answered. "It's really simple. All we have to do is to make Brandis look like a belligerent tyrant. The off-worlders are going to be armed with better weapons than arrows and all this junk. If we can make it seem as if Brandis has initiated hostilities against the off-worlders, they will have no choice but to retaliate. And we'll help them to do it. Then, with Brandis gone, I can take over the colony."

"Let's try again," Crystal said slowly and infuriatingly. "How *exactly* are we going to do it? Try leaving out the fantasies you're indulging in when you reply."

Dave had to restrain himself. It was difficult, but somehow he managed it. "Listen carefully," he told them all. "This is what we're going to do . . ."

Captain Nicola Moore stared all around as she stood beside the *Wanderer*. It felt good breathing fresh air again, instead of the recycled stuff in the ship. There was a faint tang in the breeze, obviously from the plants and trees. For a moment, it reminded her of her father's farm in Idaho. She'd spent most of her youth working on getting away from it and into space, but there was still some of the farm girl in her. She couldn't help enjoying this, or the breeze across her exposed skin.

"It's nice, right?" asked Tsu beside her. "These Earth-type worlds always are. Even for lifetime spacers like us."

"It's fine for a little while," Moore agreed. "But I couldn't take it for too long."

"We may have to," Mason reminded her. "If we can't

fix the computer and do the rest of the repairs, we're stuck here.''

Trying to ignore the pang of pain that gave her, Moore continued to scan the area. "Still no sign of anyone. Is it possible that they *are* all dead?''

Mason held up a portable scanner. "I'm getting life-form readings,'' he informed her. "Some of them are alien creatures, but several of them look definitely human. At a guess, I'd say we're being watched.''

"That doesn't make any sense,'' Tsu objected. "If there are people out there, why wouldn't they just come over and say hello?''

Moore slapped the pistol at her belt. "Maybe they don't like guns.''

"You want us to leave them in the ship?'' asked Tsu.

"No,'' Moore answered. "This is an alien planet, and there could be anything out there. I won't endanger the crew's lives by denying them weapons. But I want everyone to be *very* reluctant to use them. Especially around humans.''

"Understood,'' Tsu agreed. "I'll pass the word along.''

Captain Moore nodded, and returned to looking around the area. The trees were behind them, tall and sturdy. They looked subtly wrong somehow, so she could tell this wasn't just some farm in New England, but not so much so that they gave you the creeps. Unlike some planets she'd visited, where the plants and trees could get aggressive.

In front of them was what looked to be a corn field. The crops were about knee-high, and growing well. This was obviously a viable colony. So . . . what was going on? Why were the inhabitants hiding?

"I'm picking up a power source,'' Mason said. He gestured. "Thataway. Very low yield, so I'd guess it's a solar array. Probably feeding the colony computer.''

"Then that's where we want to be,'' Moore decided. "If there are any people around, they're bound to be there.''

"How many of us?" Mason asked.

"Not too many," she decided. "We don't want to scare them any more than we already have. You, Tsu, and myself, I think."

Tsu nodded. "I almost hate to say it, Captain, but . . . Well, if they're hiding now, maybe they might cause trouble."

"An ambush, you mean?" the captain asked. "The same thought bothered me. But I just can't see any reason why anyone would want to hurt us."

Mason couldn't resist the bait. "You can't see why anyone would want to hide from us, either," he pointed out. "But they *are* hiding."

"Yes," she was forced to admit. "But—"

There was a sudden movement by the trees, and Nicola Moore spun around, her hand moving automatically to her pistol. She stopped as she saw that it was a human being, running toward them. He was a young teenager, and gone very native. He wore only a fur loincloth, a strip of hide around his forehead to hold his long, dark hair in check, and a knife at his belt.

"The natives are restless," Mason muttered.

"Hold it in," Moore snapped. She stepped forward, aiming to meet the new arrival.

"Look out!" the youth called. "It's a trap!"

"What?" Moore spun around. "Mason, are there other—"

Several arrows whistled from the confines of the tree. Moore noted briefly that they were about three feet long, stone-tipped, and fletched expertly, as she dashed back toward the *Wanderer* for cover. One shaft slammed into the ground close to her foot.

Tsu gave a cry, and hit the ground, an arrow through her right shoulder. Moore whirled around, grabbing the other woman and helping her to her feet. Tsu had gone pale, and there was blood flowing. Moore hauled Tsu back to the shadow of the ship; the other woman was barely conscious.

The boy who had warned them dropped to the ground with them, looking wildly back at the woods. "I think they're going," he gasped, and then turned to Mason. "I'm Dave Merrick," he added. "Are you the leader here?"

"No," Mason said gently. He had his pistol out, but hadn't fired it. He nodded toward Nicola Moore. "She is."

The youth's face creased in puzzlement. "A girl?"

"A woman," she corrected. "Let's talk inside. Akiko needs medical help; then you can tell me what the hell is going on."

She handed Tsu over to Panjit, who took the injured woman off to sick bay. Then Nicola Moore could concentrate on other matters. She spun around to glare at the boy. "I'm Captain Moore," she informed him. "Just what is going on here?"

The boy glared back at her, haughtily. Her first thought was that he was obviously unprepared to deal with a woman in charge. Typical male thinking, she knew: always assuming that they were the only ones who could do a job properly. But Dave adjusted. "I'm sorry about the trouble," he said. "It's not all of us here on Tarshish. Just a small minority, led by Will Brandis. He's afraid of you. He's convinced you mean to take over control of the planet, and he decided to get the first blow in before you could."

"Take over the planet?" asked Moore, thoroughly confused. "Why would I want to do anything like that?"

"I don't know," Dave admitted. "But Brandis is crazy. He rules the colony here through fear and intimidation. He has a small army of handpicked bullies who keep the rest of the colony in line. I was thrown out because I tried to stop him. I don't agree with the way he's been doing things. And when I heard that he was planning to attack you, I knew I couldn't just stand by and let him do it. So I came to warn you. They almost caught me as I slipped through their lines, but I managed to evade them and warn you."

"Yes," she agreed. "We owe you our thanks for that. We'd been planning on exploring the colony, to see what was going on." She shuddered at the thought that she, Tsu, and Mason might well have been killed from ambush if they had tried their walk.

"Right," agreed Mason. "We owe you our lives, kid." He grinned at the youth.

Dave grinned back. "What else could I do?" he asked. "I couldn't just let them kill you."

Mason turned to Nicola Moore. "Well, what are we going to do now, Captain?" He emphasized the title slightly, putting her on the spot. "It doesn't look like we're going to get any cooperation from the folks here."

"Not while Brandis is in charge," Dave agreed hastily. "But the rest of us aren't like that. We'd love to be your friends, Captain. If only I were still in charge here, but I'm not."

"In charge?" Moore was totally confused. "You were in charge of this colony?"

"Until Brandis led his rebellion," Dave answered. "I didn't want to hurt one of my own, so I didn't fight back until it was too late. Then I was thrown out of the group."

"*You* were in charge?" she asked, unbelieving. "Surely there was somebody older running things?"

"Older?" Dave shook his head. "*I'm* the oldest. That's why I was in charge."

"*You're* the oldest?" This was getting weirder and weirder all the time. "What about your parents?"

"Oh." Dave had been as puzzled as she was, but now he realized what she meant. "They're dead," he replied. "They were all killed seven years ago. We're what's left."

"A bunch of kids in charge of a planet?" Mason muttered.

Captain Nicola Moore stared at Dave. No adults alive . . . Kids running this world . . . Well, at least some things were starting to make sense. It did explain why they hadn't

been able to detect power transmissions or communications, and why the natives were behaving in such a strange
fashion. If they were just kids here, they would naturally
be behaving a little oddly.

"You've been on your own for seven years?" she asked,
appalled. "Just kids? And you *survived?*"

"Tricky little devils, aren't they?" Mason said with a
grin.

This complicated matters considerably for them. Moore
couldn't help feeling dismayed. She'd been hoping for help
here. Now it looked like there wasn't any possible help.
Not only that, but there was a bunch of kids armed with
bows and arrows which they clearly knew how to use, and
who were determined to wage war on them.

She'd had better days . . .

CHAPTER 10

NICOLA MOORE IMMEDIATELY called a general meeting. Though she preferred simply giving orders and making certain they were obeyed, there were times when she had to explain herself. And, if she was honest with herself, get some feedback from the crew. She might be in charge, but she was under no illusion that she knew everything.

Captain Moore kept Dave close at hand. It was partially out of gratitude for his warning—which might well have saved several lives—and partially because she wasn't entirely sure that she trusted him. Not that she had any reason to actively distrust him; it was just her innate suspicious nature. Maybe he was telling the whole truth, but it could do no harm right now if she assumed that he wasn't.

Panjit was the last to arrive, looking disturbed, as usual. "How's Akiko?" she asked him as he entered.

"Doing well," the medic replied. "The arrow came out

cleanly, and I dressed the wound. I gave her some medication for the pain, so she's sleeping right now."

"Good." Nicola was relieved. She liked Tsu, and felt better knowing she wasn't suffering too much. She turned to the crew. "Right, we've got complications. But what else is new? Dave here tells me that there are no adults on this world. They were all killed seven years ago. Only the children were left alive, and he's the oldest. Most of them aren't even teenagers yet."

"Good grief," muttered Warren. "How did they manage to survive?"

Moore shrugged. "Partly luck, partly organization," she answered. "But the fact is that there's nobody here who can help us."

"Help you?" Dave asked, his face falling. "Why do you need help?"

"Because our ship was damaged in space," Moore answered. "We need to repair it. And, most urgently, we need computer access." She shrugged. "It's starting to look like we may have to consider settling here after all." It really hurt her to even consider the thought.

"Damaged?" Dave echoed. "You can't take off again?"

"Oh, we could take off," Mason told him. "But we can't leave this solar system. The main drive's damaged. And without computers, we can't repair it." He slammed his fist into the bulkhead. "Damn! I don't think I could take being a dirtsider."

Dave jumped to his feet. "We have a computer!" he exclaimed.

Nicola Moore could hardly believe it. "An operational one?" she demanded eagerly, but afraid to get her hopes up.

"Yes," he replied, nodding. "Of course, it has a few problems, mostly in the area of personality. It's a teaching program."

"I wish Tsu were here," Moore muttered. "She'd know if that was good enough. But if we can check the computer out, when she recovers, maybe she can patch it into our mainframe and recover the data we need.''

"There's just one problem,'' Dave added, a crafty look in his eye. "The computer is under the control of Brandis, and he won't allow you to use it. You'd have to get him out of the way first.''

"That's not a problem, kid,'' Mason assured him.

Captain Moore shook her head. "Slow down, Mason. You can't seriously be talking about making war on children.''

Mason glared at her. "*They* started it,'' he pointed out. "Tsu's in sick bay right now because of them. They could have killed her—or any of us. I say we strike back, and hard.''

"*You* do?'' asked Moore, with a gentle irony in her voice. "Well, it's a shame that I'm the captain then, isn't it?'' She narrowed her eyes. "These kids are probably just scared and insecure. Maybe they didn't intend to hurt us.''

Mason laughed incredulously, and gestured at Dave. "He says they planned to kill us!'' he exclaimed.

"Yes,'' the captain agreed. "*He* said. No offense, kid, but I'd prefer some proof of that before I accept it as fact.''

Dave looked hurt and annoyed. "I risked my life to come and warn you about the attack,'' he pointed out. "If I go back there now, they'll kill me. Isn't that enough proof for you? Or do you want to see me shot full of arrows?''

"He's got a point,'' Panjit agreed. "I think we should listen to him.''

"So do I,'' agreed Moore. "I simply don't think we should accept everything he says as gospel. Aside from the fact that he may have his own agenda here, he's also young enough to maybe get some of the facts twisted. No offense, kid, but that's the way of it.''

"Is it?'' Dave asked, clearly more angry than hurt. "So I just risked my neck for *nothing*? Thanks a lot.''

"Not for nothing.'' She didn't want him upset, because

he was still their only guide to this planet. "If what you say is true, then we'll certainly protect you, as you tried to help us. And when we leave—*if* we leave—we'll take you with us, if you'd like. You'd probably enjoy Earth."

"No!" he exclaimed, really angry now. "This is *my* planet! I'm not leaving here!"

Nicola Moore stared at him in astonishment. "You can't want to spend the rest of your life in this place?" she exclaimed. "There's nothing here!"

"There's *everything* here," he snapped back. "This is my world, and I should be in charge here. And I will be, if you help me. Then I can help you get off this planet."

"What is it you want?" asked Mason.

"Help me to displace the tyrant Brandis," Dave said eagerly. "Once I take his place in command here, I guarantee that the colony will help you with whatever you need."

"And how do you want us to do that?" asked Moore softly.

"You have guns!" Dave said. "And, I'm sure, other weapons too! Brandis can't stand against them!"

Moore's heart fell. She'd been afraid he'd ask for that. "Start a war for you?" she asked. "It's out of the question. Aside from any kind of ethical problems involved in overthrowing a native government, you're asking us to fire— and maybe kill—kids." She shook her head. "No way."

Mason growled in his throat. "Captain," he snapped, "I think we should *all* consider what he's asking. It might be our only way off this planet. Maybe you like the thought of dirt between your toes for the rest of your life, but I don't. And I don't think that many of the crew do, either." There was a murmur of agreement with him. "If making war on kids is what we have to do—well, then, we have to do it."

Nicola Moore was annoyed. Number one, she didn't like her decisions being questioned. Number two, she didn't like

Mason's tone at all. "*I* decide on what we have to do," she reminded him. "This is not a democracy. And if our only way off this planet is over the dead bodies of children . . . well, which of you thinks that's a price worth paying?"

There was no direct answer to that, of course. None of them was quite up to the level of wanting to advocate killing kids. But she could read their mood. They were desperate for a solution. Even if the majority backed her stance right now, it could all change in a couple of days. They were bound to start getting antsy on a world with nothing to do, and a possible hope of escape staring at them from the forests. She had to keep them occupied.

"I want a work detail set to repairing the drive chamber," she ordered. "If there is a way off this world, I want to be ready to take advantage of it. And I want Valdez's still dismantled and the parts recycled."

"Captain!" Mason protested. "That's not fair!"

"That's an order, Mason! Get rid of it!" She glared around the room, daring anyone to disobey a direct order.

Panjit chimed in. "He's right, Captain. We're all pretty much dying of boredom as it is. What's the harm of a little drink now and then?"

"What's the harm?" parroted Captain Moore, incredulous. "One crew member is dead because of that stupid still, and I won't tolerate any more alcohol-related accidents aboard this ship. Is that clear?"

"Crystal," snarled Mason.

Moore erupted. "And one more thing, Mason. I promise you the minute we set foot back on Earth I'll convene a courtmartial hearing and recommend you be tried for manslaughter in the death of crewman Valdez."

"You wouldn't dare!" snarled Mason.

"Mason, you can count on it." Then she turned to address the rest of the crew. "Now, does anybody else have any problems they'd like to discuss? No? OK. Warren, Larson, you're in charge of the repairs. I expect progress reports and I want to see that still gone." She glanced at Dave. What to do with him? "Panjit, you look after the boy. See that he gets fed and somewhere to sleep. Anyone that isn't immediately needed for repair detail, I want two of you on watch at the hatch. Vishinsky and Lloyd, you take the first detail. Pistols, of course, but don't fire at anyone or anything unless you are directly threatened, understand? I don't want to start a war here, whatever those kids want." She gave them all a final glare, and then left the room. She wanted to check on Akiko, and then she needed to be alone to think.

Mason was fuming as the door closed behind Captain Moore. He'd had plenty of trouble in the past with her being in command, but she'd really gone off the deep end now. Couldn't she see how she was endangering them all?

"*She's* the one you picked to lead you?" the native boy asked, hardly hiding the sneer in his voice.

"We didn't *pick* her," Mason growled. "She was appointed before we left Earth."

Dave shrugged. "Maybe you should unappoint her," he suggested.

"She's the captain," Larson said firmly. "We do what she orders. That's our way. I don't know how it is here on this planet, but when someone's in charge, you do as they tell you."

"Even when their orders are wrong?" asked Dave innocently. "If *I'd* obeyed orders, I wouldn't have told you about the raid. And maybe some of you would be dead now. Maybe you shouldn't obey wrong orders either."

Mason's eyes narrowed. The kid was talking mutiny, of course. The thought didn't bother him much. Not nearly as much as being tried for manslaughter and confined to a military prison for the next fifty years. No, he had no choice. He had to push Moore aside. But he couldn't do it alone. Larson, he figured, being a woman, would stick by the captain. So would some of the others. But there were enough like himself, who chafed under her rigid command and would welcome a change. "It's not her orders I object to," he lied. "It's just that I don't really see the need to destroy the still. It's bad for morale. And god knows that after all these years out in space we could all use a little morale booster now and then."

Panjit lamented, "I just don't see that there's really a need to destroy it."

"The need," Larson pointed out, "is that Captain Moore ordered it."

"She's just being vindictive," Mason suggested. "She doesn't want us to have anything to remind us of home."

Dave obviously didn't know what a still was; he was just a kid, so they couldn't have anything like that here. But he had obviously seen an opening. "And you will obey her, even if it harms everyone else?" he asked. "She must command great loyalty."

"I don't see why we should destroy the still," agreed Lloyd. "I mean, if we *are* stuck here, what else are we going to do to pass the time? I'll need something to take my mind of this dirtball planet."

"Then you'll have to find something else," Larson said coldly. "I'm obeying orders." She turned to Warren. "Come along. We'd better get started." She strode from the room.

Warren hesitated, and turned back in the doorway. "I'll talk to her," he said quietly. "I'm sure she'll come around."

Mason hoped so. Those two were an item, and Warren could apply a good deal of emotional leverage if he was smart. The rest of the crew started to disperse to their assigned duties. Mason hung back, wanting to talk with Panjit and the boy. He knew that Panjit would be on his side, and the boy was their only key to getting off this planet. As soon as the three of them were alone, he asked the youth:

"If you were back in charge again, could you gain us access to the computer?"

"Of course," Dave assured him. "But the only way to do that would be to displace Brandis. And your *captain* has decided not to do that." He gave Mason a penetrating look. "Is it easy for you to take orders from a woman? No man on this planet would ever do that."

Mason flushed. "It's not quite that simple," he growled. The problem was that it did rankle him that he was taking orders from that woman. He'd never liked her, with her aloof ways, and the way she never relaxed like the rest of them. She didn't drink, and didn't seem to have a sex drive, either. A cold fish, through and through. Inhuman, that's what she was. And now she was tossing away their only chance of ever getting away from this place and back into space again. Maybe she had the majority of the crew behind her for now, but it wouldn't last. Stuck dirtside for any length of time, a spacer would get really unhappy.

Panjit gave Mason a perceptive look. "You are thinking what?" he asked.

"I am thinking that maybe the captain likes it here," Mason said. "Maybe enough to want to stay. And we could . . . arrange for that to happen."

"Ah." Panjit caught on. "Leave her behind, you mean? But would the crew allow that?"

"Some wouldn't," Mason admitted. "If they knew. But if they didn't . . ." He spread his hands. "I'm sure they'd go along with the majority if it was a done deal."

Dave grinned, obviously catching on. "You are thinking of leaving her here when you go?" he asked. "She could be useful. She's quite . . . pretty."

"Only on the outside, kid," Mason told him. "Inside, she's as cold as a stone."

"Stones can be warmed," Dave replied.

Mason chuckled. He had to admire the kid's moxy. "Good luck, then. As far as I'm concerned, she's our gift to you. Now, we have to talk about what we can do to get you back into power again, so we can get access to that computer. It's our only hope of getting off this planet.''

"You are not as squeamish as your captain about killing . . . children?" Dave asked him.

"If it's my ticket out of here, I'll do what it takes," Mason assured him. "If this Brandis character stands in our way . . ." He tapped his pistol. "He'd either better be prepared to move out of the way, or else I'll move him. It's that simple."

"Good," said Dave happily. "Then I think we can definitely help one another here." He held out his hand. "You help to return me to power, and I will help you to leave this planet." He licked his lips. "And I will keep your captain. I am displeased with the woman I have now. She would make a good replacement."

Mason laughed. "Kid, you're taking on trouble, if you ask me, but it's your neck. I'd advise you not to let her near any weapons, though."

"She won't need weapons," Dave said.

Mason laughed again. This kid was crazy, but he was just what they needed to get the ship repaired again, and to leave Captain Moore behind. Talk about killing two birds with one stone.

And he, of course, would become the new captain . . .

CHAPTER 11

JENNA STILL WASN'T convinced that Will had made the right decision by having everyone hide from the newcomers. But she loved and trusted him, so she buried her own doubts. Well, to an extent, anyway.

While the others had gone into the jungle with the babies to hide out for as long as necessary, Jenna had snuck back to the edge of the trees to watch. Will didn't know that she'd planned this, and she'd avoided a problem with him by carefully not telling him. Jenna was a little worried that the intruders might have some high-tech way of detecting her, but she was confident that she would be able to escape from them if they came after her. After all, this was her home, and not theirs. There were plenty of ways to lose pursuers in the jungle without harming them. The sticky trees, for example. Their vines would tangle up the unwary. They could spend hours trying to get free of those.

But she *had* to see the visitors. Ms. Pringle was keeping an eye on them using her flying eyes, of course, but that was high-tech stuff, and Jenna knew that the Earth folks might be able to detect and dispose of that a lot faster than they could get rid of her. So she wanted to be there, just in case. She settled into the crook of a tree and watched as the scout ship landed.

It was very impressive, she had to admit. A lot of smoke and flames, and this thing the size of a large house and shaped like a beetle bug was sitting on the edge of the corn field. She realized that whoever was flying it had carefully avoided burning the crops or landing on them. That was one good point in their favor. Eagerly, she watched to see what would happen next.

Then a hatchway opened, and several people came out. Jenna watched them carefully, and felt a pang as she saw that they were all adults. She'd been expecting it, of course, but these were the first adults she'd seen since her parents had died.

And then she almost fell out of the tree in shock. Dave came running out of the jungle about two hundred yards from her, screaming a warning at the people by the ship. To her astonishment, several arrows were fired after Dave. One of them hit one of the Earth women, and she went down. Another woman scooped her to her feet, and they all retreated to their ship, closing the hatch.

And Dave went with them.

Jenna was too amazed to react at first. What had that been all about? Dave had called: "Look out! It's a trap!" But who would have set such a trap? Certainly not Will . . .

A growing suspicion stunned her for a moment, and then she moved. She dropped from the tree and hurried through the jungle in the direction of the arrows. She moved soundlessly, as she did when hunting. She was hunting now.

After a few moments, she caught up with the retreating attackers. As she'd suspected, they were Dave's followers. Byron, Donna, and Crystal. They were laughing and joking about what they had done.

But *why* had they done it?

There was only one way to find out. Jenna trailed them, unseen and unheard, until Donna moved off from the others. Answering the call of nature, no doubt. Jenna smiled grimly; she'd be answering something else in a moment. Jenna scurried up the closest tree, and went from branch to branch above the rest of the party and after Donna. On her way she sliced off a length of sticky vine, carefully holding it with a leaf instead of her hand.

Donna was just starting to move back to rejoin the rest when Jenna pounced. Dropping down from the branch above her, she slammed into the smaller girl with both feet. Donna's breath exploded from her lungs as she was slammed into the ground. Jenna whipped the sticky vine around her wrists and feet, and then watched as Donna gasped and wheezed. Since this was no time for politeness, Jenna pulled her knife from its sheath and held it under Donna's nose.

"One yell from you, and I'll cut out your tongue," she promised. "And if you don't answer my questions, I'll cut it out." The fear in Donna's eyes showed that the other girl believed her threat. "Now . . . what was that attack all about?"

Donna started shaking. Obviously, she didn't want to tell; equally obviously, she didn't want to loose her tongue. Jenna sighed, and realized she was going to have to be a little nastier.

"Okay," she said. "We do this the hard way. I'm not going to cut your tongue out right away, because it would be terribly rough for me to have to interrogate you if you have to play charades to answer me. So let's start at the other end, shall we?" She grabbed Donna's left foot. "Do you have any idea how painful walking's going to be for you with several slashes in the sole?" She moved her knife into position and started to press down.

As she'd been hoping, Donna immediately said: "No, wait! I'll tell you!"

Jenna was relieved; she really didn't want to hurt the other girl. But she would if she was forced to do so. "So, again: what was that attack all about?"

"It's Dave's idea," Donna babbled quickly. "He's blaming it on Brandis, telling them that Brandis wants to kill the intruders to get them off the planet."

Jenna scowled. "But why would he do that?"

"He wants the strangers to help him get rid of Brandis, so Dave can take over leadership," Donna explained. "It should be his by right, you know."

"Idiot," Jenna said without sympathy. "There's no such right on this planet. Dave would make a lousy leader, and this stupid little plan of his just proves it." She considered her options and then stood up. "Right, I'm off. You can scream for help if you like now. But I'd be wary of what you tell your friends. If you admit you've told me what Dave's up to, they might not be very happy with you. And I can guarantee you that Dave will be *very* unhappy." With a final grin to hammer home her point, she turned and ran back toward the ship.

She wasn't too surprised when Donna didn't immediately call for help. She was going to have to do a bit of fast thinking first, and she really wasn't equipped for it.

Meanwhile, Jenna had some thinking of her own to do right now. Dave was inside the Earth people's ship, spreading lies about Will and the rest of them. Would the strangers believe him? That had been quite an act he'd put on, and he could be quite convincing when he wanted to be. Why would the visitors not accept his story as true?

Which could cause a definite problem. If the scouts believed that Will had ordered an attack on them, then they might just decide to retaliate, which was obviously what Dave was hoping for. They might just kill Will. The thought made Jenna sick, and she knew that she couldn't let that happen. There was only one thing for her to do: she had to make certain that the Earth people heard the truth.

She didn't like her decision, but there was no other way that she could see. She refused to give in to her fear, and, now she'd decided what she was doing, she headed directly for the ship.

Close up, it looked even more insectlike and terrifying. Swallowing, she made her way to where she'd seen the hatch earlier. It was still closed. Obviously, the crew wasn't chancing any more attacks. How did one get inside? There weren't any controls, and even if there were, she wouldn't know how to use them. Taking her knife from its sheath, she used the bone handle to rap loudly on the hatch. Somebody inside was bound to hear her.

The door hissed open, and two guns were thrust into her face. Trying to be brave, Jenna held up her hands. "I come in peace," she said. "I want to talk to your leader. You've been hearing lies about us."

The two guards looked at her and then at each other. "You'd better come in," one said. "But I'll take that knife, first. Gently."

Jenna handed it over, and then sprang into the hatchway. "I must talk with your leader," she insisted.

"This way," the same man said. The other closed the hatch behind her. Jenna nodded, and set out.

Mason was still musing on how he could achieve his aims. There had to be some way to "accidentally" leave the captain behind. Once they were in space, Mason felt confident he could convince the waverers that the episode had been unfortunate, but inescapable. The truth was, Captain Moore had made no close allies on board and no friends. She would not be missed.

But how to leave the captain here in the first place? That was the problem.

Lloyd opened the door, and gestured a young girl into the room. Mason looked at her with interest. She looked like the distaff version of Dave, but she was definitely more interesting. She looked like she'd stepped out of one of the old vids about jungle girls—a furry bikini, a sheath for her knife at her side, her hair long and tied back with a thong. She couldn't be more than sixteen, but she was very striking. Even Panjit, who normally didn't pay much attention to women, stared at her.

So, Mason noted, did Dave—only with annoyance and shock. Interesting . . .

The girl raised an eyebrow, staring back at their other visitor. "Been spreading lies as usual?" she asked him. Then she turned to Mason. "Are you the leader here?"

"Not yet," he replied. "Why?"

The girl pointed at Dave. "He has been filling you with lies."

"Has he indeed?" Mason asked softly. He looked at the young man, and saw immediately in his eyes that the girl was telling the truth. But the boy didn't cave in.

"Of course she would claim that," Dave said, trying to act offended and noble. "She is Brandis's girl. Obviously, since his attack failed, he's trying to lure you out for another attempt."

Mason smiled. It was a plausible story, but he'd already seen the truth in Dave's eyes. "Stow it," he advised. Then he turned back to the girl. "And what *is* the truth?" he asked. "What is it that you and this Brandis want with us?"

"Simply to be left alone," she replied. "Go away."

Mason shook his head. "It's not that simple."

"It is," she insisted. "We will not harm you, but we want nothing to do with you."

"One of you has already harmed one of us," Panjit pointed out.

"One of *his* followers," the girl replied with a sneer in

Dave's direction. "So that you would better believe his story."

It made sense. Mason eyed Dave with interest. He'd cooked up a good plan to back up his story, and Mason couldn't help admiring that. Even now that he'd been caught out, he simply stood there, arms folded, waiting to see what would happen. "A power play, eh?" Mason asked, chuckling softly. "You're trying to take over the colony, Dave?"

"As you are trying to take over this ship," the youth answered.

"Good point," Mason agreed. "Well, I don't really care *who* runs this colony, just as long as we get off it." He glanced at Panjit, and nodded toward the medical pouch the man wore, and then looked back at the girl. Panjit, standing close beside her, gave a slight nod to show that he'd understood.

"Listen, kid," Mason told the girl, "you're a nice-looking girl and all. But if your boyfriend won't help us, and Dave here will, I know which side of this power struggle I'm on."

"Help?" the girl echoed, puzzled. "What do you mean?"

She got no further, because Panjit had his trank spray out, and dosed her with it. Her eyes glazed over and she collapsed. Panjit caught her before she could hit the floor.

"Nicely done," Mason said approvingly. "Maybe you'd better find her a bed in sick bay. You'd probably better tie her down, too. Lloyd, hand me her knife. We'll have to report this to the captain. I'll tell her the girl attacked me with her knife as we were talking, and we have to keep her confined." He glanced at Dave as Panjit struggled out of the room carrying the unconscious girl. "So it was your pals who attacked us? Are they likely to attack us again if we leave the ship?"

"Not as long as I'm with you," Dave replied, staring at him with caution.

"Relax," Mason assured him with a laugh. "I'm not annoyed at you. Quite the reverse, if anything. You're a quick thinker; my kind of guy. And ambitious, just like me. I think we'll get along just fine. You scratch my back, and I'll scratch yours. I don't see any need to let the captain know it's safe out there. In fact . . ." An idea occurred to him. "Maybe we can stage another little attack when we're ready. One that will take the captain from us."

"I don't want to kill her," Dave said stubbornly. "I want her."

Mason laughed again. "You're likely to regret that decision. But it's your choice. All you have to do is to injure her. Panjit and I will say she's dead, and nobody here will know any different. Then you can keep her, and we'll leave."

Dave nodded. "That sounds workable. But first, you must help me to dispose of Brandis. With him out of the way, I can take over the computer that you need."

"Fine," Mason agreed. He reached into a locker and pulled out a pistol. Tossing it to Dave, he said: "It's very simple to use. Point it at your foe and pull the trigger."

"I know how it works," Dave replied. "I've seen historical vids about the Wild West."

"Hi-ho Silver," grunted Mason, with a smile. This was all working out very well indeed. "Lloyd, let Dave out so that he can get his team ready. Then you'd better come back here quickly. We don't want the captain to know you've been gone." He chuckled. "When we go looking for this computer, she's going to get a very nasty shock . . ."

CHAPTER 12

WILL WAS WORRIED. The colonists were all well hidden in the woods. Unless the strangers had some sort of tracking devices, they would never find anyone. If they did, there was nothing that Will could do about it, so he simply ignored the possibility. What was worrying him was that Ms. Pringle had been left unguarded. Perhaps she was right, and she could defend herself against the Earth people. But what if they had more sophisticated computers themselves by now? It was quite possible.

And he was worried about Jenna. She wasn't with the group, and she hadn't told him she'd be missing. He was well used to her by now, and knew exactly what this meant: she was disregarding his instructions. He was almost certain she'd be watching the scouts from some hidden vantage in the jungle. This irritated him, but he knew there wasn't much he could do about it. He wasn't exactly worried for her—if anyone could take care of herself, it was Jenna, after all—but he was worried that the Earth people might find her. Then what would happen?

It was his job to look after his people, he knew. But it was also his job to look after Jenna and Ms. Pringle. Making up his mind, Will went to Amber. "I have to go back and check on the intruders," he told her. "Until I get back, you're in charge."

"Check on Jenna, you mean," Amber answered with a cheeky grin. "You know she's watching them, don't you?"

"Yes," he admitted with a sigh. "She never was very good at taking orders."

"That's one of the reasons you like her," Amber said. "Go on. I'll watch things here. You straighten her out." She grinned. "Maybe a few good smacks to her backside. She might even enjoy it."

Will blushed at the thought, nodded his thanks, and hurried back down the trail. He was almost certain that Jenna was fine. But he'd prefer to be one hundred percent certain. As for Ms. Pringle, well, there was simply no telling. Even though he tried not to be anxious, he couldn't help himself.

And what about Dave and his bunch of social misfits? Would they steer clear of the Earth ship or not? There were just too many questions, and not enough answers. He increased his speed, determined to find out all that he could.

Nicola Moore studied the ground outside of the ship closely with power binoculars. There was no sign of trouble, though that was no guarantee of the absence of trouble. It could just be well hidden. On the other hand, they couldn't stay here forever. Larson had reported that the repairs were going well, and they really needed to know if they could access the mainframe.

"Okay," she decided finally. "Mason, Lloyd, Vishinsky—you're with me. Dave, you lead the way. I want everyone alert for trouble, but there's to be no firing unless I say so."

"Not even if they start shooting?" Mason objected.

"Not even then." Moore scowled at him. "Are you okay with that, or should I leave you behind?"

"I'm okay," he assured her.

"Fine. Let's go." She led the way out, and made certain the lock was sealed behind them. She left her pistol conspicuously holstered. There was no point in provoking trouble. She wished they had some zen-armor with them, but there had been no real reason to expect trouble like this. While scouting could be dangerous, usually their ship could just take them away from potential trouble. Ravenous monsters attacking scouts were a staple of vid entertainment, but the reality was that the universe just wasn't that nasty. More scouts were killed through accidents and carelessness. Like Valdez . . .

Dave led the way across the field, and then through the abandoned buildings of the small town. Captain Moore saw evidence of the destruction that had killed the adults seven years earlier, but some of the houses had been patched and were evidently being lived in. Despite all odds, these kids seemed to have made something of their lives. She couldn't help admiring them for it, even if they were so inexplicably hostile.

The way led to a small valley outside the settlement. Nicola Moore's hopes rose as she realized the two buildings here were made of metal. They were parts of the holds of the original starships! There might well be materials that they could use here, along with the colony computer! This could be their ticket off this world.

If they weren't attacked again . . .

Jenna awoke slowly, her cloudy mind gradually slipping back into focus. She blinked and opened her eyes. When she tried to sit up, she discovered that she was tied down. As her vision cleared, she realized she was on a bed, with straps firmly holding her ankles and wrists.

What was going on? Her memory struggled to surface, and then she recalled being attacked and obviously drugged. The men she'd spoken to had known Dave was lying, but they simply didn't care. They were planning to hurt, and possibly kill, Will! She had to get out of here, to warn Will and stop them! She tried to pull free of the restraints, without luck.

"They're stronger than you are."

Jenna managed to twist around to see the man who'd drugged her. He had to be the ship's doctor, and he was staring down at her thoughtfully.

"Let me go," she begged. "I have to warn Will. They're planning to kill him!"

"I'm sorry," the doctor answered, shaking his head. "I can't do that. We've struck a bargain with Dave. We get rid of your Will, and he gets rid of our captain. That way, we both get what we want."

"But Dave's not right in the head!" Jenna protested. "He wants to take over the colony and become a tyrant."

The doctor shrugged. "That really doesn't bother me," he admitted. "All I want to do is to get off this planet. Will won't help us, but Dave is going to. That makes choosing sides really simple for me. He's taken the captain off to your computer right now, with Mason."

Jenna collapsed back, frustrated. All her struggles had done was to cut skin off her wrists. "You mentioned before that you needed help," she said slowly. "What do you mean?"

"Our ship was damaged," he answered. "We need help to repair it, so we can leave again."

Jenna blinked, and then realized what he was saying. "You didn't come here to take control of the colony, then? Or to force us to return to Earth with you?"

The doctor snorted. "Of course not. We don't give a damn about you. We just want our ship repaired, so we can leave."

"Oh." Jenna thought quickly. "In that case, I'm sure I can convince Will that we should help you. We were only hiding because we were afraid of you."

He looked down at her and then shrugged again. "Maybe you're telling me the truth," he said. "Maybe it's a trick just to get free. Either way, I don't care. We've made our bargain already. Would your Will agree to get rid of our captain for us, too?"

Jenna couldn't understand him. "Why do you wish to remove your leader?"

"Because she's a fool and a heartless automaton!" the doctor snarled. "She wants to control us like thoughtless children. It's her fault we're in this mess. If she'd only allowed Valdez to make his liquor in the open, there wouldn't have been any explosion."

Jenna didn't have a clue as to what he meant, but it was hardly important. "No," she confessed. "Will would not help you to harm your Captain. We do not harm other human beings. It is against our rules."

He smiled pityingly down at her. "It's a shame that it's not against ours, too, isn't it?"

"Yes," said a fresh voice from behind him. He started to turn, but his eyes glazed over, and he collapsed to the floor. "But you're lucky it's against mine," the woman added.

Jenna stared at her in hope. She wore a bandage about her right shoulder, and was obviously the person who'd been wounded in Dave's attack earlier. Using her one good arm, she started to unfasten the straps about Jenna's wrists. "Panjit was always an idiot," she commented. "He thought I was still out cold. I've been listening for a while. My name's Tsu, by the way."

The first strap was free, and Jenna used her hand to untie her other wrist and then sat up, rubbing at the raw spots. "I'm Jenna. Thank you for your help."

"Well, it sounds to me like we need to help each other,"

Tsu told her, as they freed Jenna's feet. "You want to save your Will, and I want to save my Captain. The problem is, I don't know how many of the crew are in this mutiny with Panjit."

"A tall one named Mason," Jenna replied. "And a guard named Lloyd. Those I know of." She lifted the unconscious doctor to the bed. "How long will this drug keep him unconscious?"

"A couple of hours," Tsu answered as they strapped Panjit down. "By then, things should be over."

Jenna nodded. "Can we get out of this ship without being seen by the guards?" she asked.

"Emergency exit," Tsu answered. "But where is your computer? Panjit said that's where Dave has taken Captain Moore. It's the likeliest place for an ambush."

"I can get us there," Jenna informed her. "But we had better hurry."

"We're going to need weapons," Tsu objected.

Jenna gave her a sharp look. "Didn't you hear what I said earlier? We do not hurt other people. I do not intend to use a weapon on any human being."

"Girl, that's very noble," Tsu answered, as she took a pistol from Panjit. "But there are other human beings who wouldn't hesitate to use a weapon on you. Pacifism's all very well, but it takes two people for it to work. And it only takes one person to declare war." She led the way to the door. "Now come on."

Nicola Moore walked carefully into the corridor of the old cargo hold. It was in very good shape, she noted. She'd also spotted the flying eye that had watched their approach. The computer knew that they were coming.

There was a tall, dignified woman waiting for her. Since all of the adults in the colony had been killed, Nicola knew this had to be a hologram. "The main computer, I assume?" she asked. The others joined her where she stood.

The image inclined its head slightly. "I am generally referred to as Ms. Pringle," she replied. "I am the teaching program."

Captain Moore nodded. "You're what's kept these kids alive for so long?"

"No," Ms. Pringle answered. "They kept themselves alive. I am the one who has taught them the skills they need."

With a grin, Nicola said: "You're better than any of the teachers I ever had then."

"Let's get to the point," Mason grumbled.

She was irritated with him, but he was correct. "Well, maybe we'll continue the social pleasantries later. Right now, I need access to your programming core."

Ms. Pringle shook her head. "I am afraid I cannot allow that."

"I told you," Dave said smugly. "Brandis has made sure you won't get the help you need."

"You're just a hologram," Moore pointed out to Ms. Pringle. "You can't exactly stop me. And I'm sure there must be something in your programming somewhere that prevents you from killing a human being."

"There is," agreed Ms. Pringle with a slight frown. "But I don't need to kill you to stop you. I can make it . . . very unpleasant for you if you attempt to alter my programming."

"Well, I'm sorry," Moore apologized. "I really have no choice. We need to know if you can be adapted to help us out."

"If all you need is help," Ms. Pringle said, "then perhaps I can do that. As long as it does not endanger the colony, I am willing to work with you."

"It's a trick!" Dave said. "She's lying! She's been programmed by Brandis! She's planning on killing you. Don't listen to her!"

Ms. Pringle stared at him with her lip curling slightly.

"Dave Merrick, you were always an unpleasant boy," she said. "You have not changed while you've been growing up."

Nicola Moore didn't know which of them to believe. Both of them made good sense, only they were contradicting one another. She didn't know which to believe, but there was a simple way out of this—taking control of the computer herself. "Turn your controls over to me voluntarily," she ordered Ms. Pringle. "Or I shall be forced to take action."

"I cannot do that," Ms. Pringle repeated firmly. "And I would strongly caution you against doing anything foolish."

"Says you," Moore snapped, and she moved forward.

Something hit her with all the force of a lightning bolt.

CHAPTER 13

JENNA WAS AMAZED that Tsu almost kept up with her, despite her wound. As they dashed along the valley toward the schoolhouse, Jenna heard the sound of an electrical discharge. Ms. Pringle was defending herself! The plotters must have struck already.

She hurtled through the doorway, and took in the scene in a glance. The woman captain was down on the floor, dazed and very shaken. Her pistol had gone flying. Mason and Lloyd, the two mutineers, moved forward, but not toward the computer.

"While she's stunned," Mason said. "Dave, your people can take her. We'll tell them back at the ship that the computer fried her."

"What?" Captain Moore asked, shaking her head, trying to clear it. She seemed to be badly affected by the blast.

"And what will you tell them about *us*?" Tsu demanded, panting, as she arrived. She held her pistol leveled at Mason. "Your mutiny's over."

Mason snarled and fired at her. Jenna was stunned: these people were really ready to kill one another! What kind of a world did they come from? The shot snarled past her ear, and she dove for cover.

"Ms. Pringle!" she yelled. "Stop them!"

The computer didn't need to reply. Jenna saw the angry look in the holoteacher's eyes, and another blast of electricity struck Mason. His body jerked from the shock, the pistol flying from his spasming fingers. With a cry, he dropped to the floor beside his intended victim, the captain.

Lloyd, the remaining guard, backed away, obviously terrified of being felled by a similar blast. Tsu looked nervous, too, and Jenna couldn't blame her. She'd ordered the computer to stop the fighting, and it might decide to zap Tsu as well.

Dave snarled angrily. "You're lousing up my plans!" he yelled at Jenna.

"Good," she snapped back. "I won't let you harm Will—or the colony."

Growling incoherently, he leaped toward her. Jenna abruptly realized that he had one of the pistols, too, and he was pulling it out to use on her.

One of their own, caught up in this off-worlder madness!

Jenna didn't react fast enough. Dave brought the gun up, his finger tightening on the trigger. She saw that it was aimed at her head, but she was too shocked to move out of the way. She realized that she was looking at her own death.

And then Dave screamed as an arrow slammed into his hand. The pistol went flying, and Dave clutched his shattered hand, which was bleeding all over the floor. Jenna whirled around, but she already knew who she'd see.

Will sighed and shook his head, a second arrow ready to fire if it was needed. "Jenna, Jenna," he said. "Out making friends and you didn't invite me."

"I knew you'd come anyway," she told him, running to him and giving him a quick hug.

Will glared at Tsu and then Lloyd. "Both of you had better put those guns away," he said firmly. "Otherwise Ms. Pringle and I will be *very* upset."

Tsu obeyed instantly. Lloyd hesitated for a second, then looked down at the dazed Mason. Making his mind up, he slipped his gun back into its holster.

Will sighed heavily. "I don't like this," he told Jenna. "I've already been forced to break our prime law. I've had to hurt Dave."

"To save my life," Jenna answered. "He was going to kill me."

"That's the only thing that's keeping me sane," Will informed her. "Only to save you would I ever have hurt another human being." He gave her a quick kiss on the cheek, and then slipped his arrow back into its quiver and slung his bow over his shoulder. "Ms. Pringle, what about the two you shocked?"

"They will recover," the holoteacher promised. "They are simply disoriented and hurting. Dave, however, requires medical attention."

"He'll get it when I'm good and ready," Will snapped. He ignored the whimpering boy, and turned to Jenna. "Now, what the hell is going on here?"

Several hours later, an agreement had been worked out. Jenna patted Will's hand proudly, as the last details were sorted out. It had been a hectic time. Dave was in the *Wanderer*'s sick bay, his hand bandaged. Mason, Lloyd, and Panjit were locked together in one of the crew rooms. The rest of the crew had all proclaimed that they knew nothing at all about any mutiny. They had, however, removed all remnants of a device that was called a "still," obviously to appease their captain and to prove their loyalty.

Captain Moore had turned out not to be so bad after all,

once they'd gotten to know her. She was interested only in getting her ship repaired. Despite Will's fears, she had absolutely no interest in taking over the colony.

"What?" she asked, laughing. "I have enough trouble with just this damned crew. I don't need to be looking after a bunch of kids, too. It seems to me that you guys don't need any outside help at all."

She and Will had managed to agree on repairs. Ms. Pringle was certain she could access the data from the *Wanderer*'s broken computer, and repairing the drive should then be quite simple. A bit of metal smelting was all that would be required. Captain Moore's crew would build a forge, which the colony could then use once the ship was gone.

"Now," Captain Nicola Moore said, relaxing slightly. "There're just three things to be taken care of." The three of them and Akiko Tsu were sitting in the schoolroom, with Ms. Pringle. "First, what are we going to do with Merrick?" She looked at Will carefully.

"I don't know," he admitted. "Personally, I'd like to kill him with my bare hands. But there has been enough violence already."

"Then I have a suggestion," the captain replied. "I'll take him back to Earth with us. He did try and either kidnap or kill me, so I'm within my rights to arrest him. There, he'll be sent to a prison, and taught a useful job. Who knows, he may even prefer Earth to Tarshish. Is that okay?"

Will looked at Jenna, who nodded firmly. Getting Dave Merrick out of the colony was a great idea. "Fine," Will agreed.

"Second thing," Captain Moore said. "Why don't you all come with us, back to Earth? The *Wanderer* isn't very big, but I'm sure we could fit you all in with a little crowding. I mean, you've done incredibly well to survive here as you have, but . . . Well, it's a dangerous place. Those creatures that killed your parents could come back.''

''They will,'' Jenna said flatly. ''I've been studying them. They're like some forms of Earth insects. They hatch from eggs, grow quickly, and then migrate, consuming everything in their path. They then mate, lay eggs, and die. Because they're so large, and complex, it takes a number of years for the eggs to incubate and the monsters to break out. Then they start another wave.'' She shrugged. ''I don't know how long it'll take, but they will be back.''

''Come with us, then,'' Tsu urged. ''Get away before they come back. And there's so much you can do on Earth! There's so much freedom you'll have, so many possibilities. If you stay here, it will always be a struggle for survival.''

''Perhaps,'' agreed Will. ''But Tarshish is our *home*. Our parents brought us here, and they tried to build us a home. They died here, but not their hope. That still lives . . . in us. We've struggled, yes, but we've built a place we love.'' He held up a hand. ''I'm not making a decision for the whole colony. We will hold a meeting, and everyone will be given a choice. If anyone wants to do so, they will be welcome to go with you.''

''But I don't think many will,'' Jenna added, holding Will's hand proudly. ''This is where we belong. Monsters and all. Next time they come, we'll be ready. We have food stockpiled, and we'll have more warning next time. Ms. Pringle is monitoring constantly for them. We'll figure out what to do about the monsters eventually. They won't ruin our home forever.''

Captain Moore smiled. ''Well, you kids have plenty of courage, that's all I can say. I almost envy you—except I think you're crazy for ever wanting to live on a planet in the first place.'' She leaned forward slightly. ''You could come on the *Wanderer* anyway. There are stars to see, planets to explore, people to meet. A million and one incredible sights.''

"Thank you," Will said. "But I can see all I want right here." He squeezed Jenna's hand.

"Young love," the captain said, snorting slightly. "There's no arguing with it."

"Maybe you should try it yourself before you get too old," Tsu told her.

"Take your own advice," Captain Nicola Moore snapped back, but with a smile to take the sting from it.

"You said that there were three points," Will gently reminded her.

"Oh, yes, right," the captain said. "Now that we're all done, what's the chance of getting a home-cooked meal? I am *sick* of replicated food!"

Will felt really happy for the first time in what seemed to be days. The strain had been eating at him, and it was so good for it to be over. He'd brought back the colony, and they'd all been given the option of going back with the *Wanderer*. He hadn't been surprised when only Dave's breakaway group had decided to take up the opportunity.

"And we're better off without them," Jenna said firmly.

Will was inclined to agree. Without the troublemakers, the colony was focused again. They had all helped with the building and operation of the forge, and it took only two days for the broken generator on the ship to be repaired. Tomorrow, the *Wanderer* would lift off, and they would be alone again.

To his surprise, he almost regretted it. He had grown quite fond of Captain Nicola Moore. She was a pig-headed woman sometimes, but she was clever, adaptable, and even rather intelligent . . . for an adult. She needed to learn to bend a little, but otherwise she was rather nice.

"I hope you're not thinking about starting to date older women," Jenna said, with mock seriousness.

Will blushed at the thought. "No!" he exclaimed. "It's just that . . . Well, I think I'm going to miss the captain."

"Me too," Jenna agreed. "But she's getting very restless, being confined on a single planet this long."

"Damned right," Captain Moore said, coming to join them. "It's unnatural. For me, at least. For you . . ." She grinned. "Though I could get really addicted to your food. What was that last dish again?"

"Fuzzbat stew," Jenna replied. "Do you want the recipe?"

"Where else would I get fuzzbats?" Captain Nicola Moore smiled lazily. "My offer's still open if you change your mind."

"I know it is," Will agreed. "And you could still stay here if you change yours."

"Not likely!" The captain laughed. "We're both too set in our own ways, aren't we?"

Ms. Pringle suddenly appeared, and she looked very worried. "It's happened, Will," she reported. "The monsters are back!"

She turned on the holofeed. In the glowing globe, Will could see the black, insectlike creatures on the march again. They were tearing a path through the trees. His throat constricted, and his heart raced.

The worst time of their lives was about to start again . . .

CHAPTER 14

WILL COULD HARDLY believe the dreadful timing. Just as he'd thought their problems were over, the greatest threat of them all was back. But he couldn't afford to waste any time.

"Jenna," he ordered. "Start the recall. We have to have everyone back inside the schoolhouse *immediately*. Amber!" he yelled. "Make certain that there's enough sheepnik milk for three days! See to the babies!" He turned to Captain Moore. "Captain, get all of your crew back aboard your ship or else in here. Anyone who lags will be eaten."

"So I gathered," she responded, pulling out her communicator and giving the recall order. Then she said: "Will, think for a moment. We can get you all aboard the *Wanderer* and off-planet before those things get here. Think about it for a minute. They're going to destroy *everything* that you people have built here. You're going to be left with *nothing*. You're going to have to start again from scratch, and build it all up again. *And then they'll come back again.* It's a never-ending cycle.''

Will looked at her, disturbed by what she said.

Ms. Pringle nodded. ''She is right, Will. As long as you stay here, those monsters are going to keep ravaging this world. You'll never stop fighting. Perhaps you should consider going back to Earth with her. I know you think it would be a loss, but there is so much that Earth has to offer that you will never know here. And those babies will never know, either. By staying here, you're dooming them to the same fight and loss cycle that you're now going through.''

''This is our *home*!'' Will exclaimed. ''Okay, it may not be the best planet in the galaxy. Maybe Earth *is* better. But so what? There are probably planets even better than Earth.'' He glared at Captain Moore. ''For all its virtues, it can't keep you there, can it? Why should we then let it trap us? Even with the monsters, *here* is where we belong. If we have to fight and retreat and rebuild, then so be it. But we will not surrender to them.'' He looked at Ms. Pringle. ''When everyone arrives here, we'll hold another meeting if we have the time. Everyone will be given the same choice of whether to stay or leave. But, even if everyone else goes, I'm staying. Nobody and nothing drives me from my home.''

Jenna clasped his hand. ''And I'm staying with you,'' she vowed. He felt a surge of love for her. She might argue with him from time to time, but there was absolutely no question about her devotion and affection for him.

''More fool you, then,'' Nicola Moore answered. ''I'd better get back to my ship. I don't think those things can damage it, but I think it might be prudent to bring forward our take-off time.''

Ms. Pringle looked anguished. ''But you'll give the children time to come if they so decide?'' she begged.

"Of course," the captain promised. "We won't leave anyone behind if they want to go. You have my word on that." She handed Will one of the communication devices she always carried. "Press the small red button. That will signal us, and I'll answer. We'll hold as long as we dare. I promise."

"Thank you, Captain." Will slid the device onto his wrist. "Now, we all have work to do."

The next hour was absolute insanity. Still, Will had planned a long time for this day, knowing that it was inevitable. Even the hunters got the recall message and hurried back. A dozen people manned the stores in the other building, sealing it against the monsters. Amber had the nursery humming, and every baby accounted for. Sheepniks were herded into the building, and all portable food was transported inside. Head counts were carried out and checked twice, to be absolutely certain that everyone was present. Will had the doors locked, and then assembled everyone in the main dining room.

"The monsters are back," he told them, even though they all knew this by now. They were all working on adrenaline, scared, but determined. "Captain Nicola Moore has again offered to take anyone who wants to leave with her on the *Wanderer*. Ms. Pringle believes that we should accept her offer, so I'll let her speak to you all."

Ms. Pringle moved forward. "The monsters are back," she said quietly, but everyone else was silent, intent on her words. "And they will be back, again and again, regularly. They will destroy whatever you have built out there. And when you rebuild, they will return and destroy it again. It makes no sense for you to live like this when you can escape it by returning to Earth.

"There will be more opportunities there for you, too. They have so much on Earth that you will never have here. If you stay on Tarshish, all you will have is a guarantee of struggle for you and your own children as long as you live.

If you go to Earth, then you can make your own lives, choose what you wish.'' She looked to Will.

He stepped forward. ''I have to confess, what Ms. Pringle says makes a lot of sense. If we stay here, we'll need to continually fight for our survival and our way of life. She's probably right that we should think about going. But I'm not leaving. This is my home, and I am a part of this world now. We can survive because we *have* survived. Even if the monsters destroy everything out there, they can't destroy what we have in here.

''And I'm not just talking about physical things,'' he added. ''I'm talking about the bonds that link us together. They may be able to kill and devour me, but they can't make me stop loving Jenna. Or any of the rest of you. Or this monster-infested planet. Maybe it isn't much, but it's my home. If any of you wish to leave, you know I won't think any the less of you for it. But I'm staying.''

''And so am I,'' Jenna added, standing firmly by his side.

''Geez,'' Amber said, rolling her eyes. ''Why do you guys have to make such a production out of everything? I'm staying, too. You're bound to have lots of kids, and I wouldn't trust you to change their diapers regularly if I didn't yell at you.''

''We're staying,'' Tiffany said firmly, clutching Bryan's hand tightly. ''It's our home, too. Even if we have to rebuild it every few years.''

''And me,'' Andrea agreed.

The whole room repeated the same statements, grinning, and shaking their fists in the air in defiance.

''They're not driving us away,'' Adam summed up for them all. ''Not the monsters, not Dave, not the *Wanderer*. Nothing will make us move.''

Will felt terribly proud of them all. He was afraid he'd embarrass himself and start crying or something. Turning to Ms. Pringle, he said while fighting the tightness in his throat: "I think you can call off the emergency now, don't you?"

"Huh?" Jenna looked at him as if he were crazy. She wasn't the only one.

"There aren't any monsters," Will said gently. "Ms. Pringle created a fake emergency. The timing was just *too* coincidental to be believable."

Ms. Pringle sighed. "I can see that I'm really going to have to give up lying to you, Will. You're getting too good at seeing through me." The alarms shut down, and the pictures of the rampaging monsters vanished.

"It was all *faked*?" Jenna said, catching on. "The monsters aren't back?"

"No," Will agreed.

Amber scowled. "Then why the heck was Ms. Pringle scaring us like that?"

Ms. Pringle coughed. "I sincerely believe that you would all be better off back on Earth," she explained. "I thought that, with the monsters on the loose again, you'd all see that and agree with me. But you didn't."

"Because you're wrong," Will said. "We wouldn't be better off on Earth. We're not just at home here, Ms. Pringle. We're a community. We're all part of each other. We all need each other, and rely on each other. It's bigger than the sum of our individual parts." He shrugged. "I know it may not make a lot of sense to a logical computer, but we're human beings, and we see things differently."

"So I perceive," Ms. Pringle said. She stared at him. "This was a faked emergency," she added. "But the next one won't be."

"I know," he agreed. "We all know. But it doesn't matter. We'll figure out some way to keep the monsters away. Maybe not the next time they attack, or the one after that, but eventually. This is our world now, and they'd better get used to it."

Ms. Pringle smiled, with obvious pride. "They're not the only ones who'd better get used to it," she replied softly. "I can see that I had better come to terms with it, too. We're all here to stay."

Epilogue

THE GALAXY IS a large place, with room for many, many colonies and many cultures. Some do no more than copy their planet of origin. Others experiment with new ways to live, to survive, and to grow. Tarshish is one of these. They have found their own home, and refuse to be driven out of it. It may not be Eden, but it is where they belong.

The colonists there are human beings, striving to create a new and different society. It is unlike any here on Earth. But they are just one small segment of the spirit of the human race, which reaches from the inner self to the outermost limits of creation.

TOR BOOKS

☑ Check out these titles from
Award-Winning Young Adult Author
NEAL SHUSTERMAN

TOR BOOKS

"A GREAT NEW TALENT. HE BLOWS MY MIND IN A FUN WAY."
—Christopher Pike

Welcome to the PsychoZone.

Where is it? Don't bother looking for it on a map. It's not a place, but a state of mind—a twisted corridor in the brain where reality and imagination collide.

But hold on tight. Once inside the PsychoZone there's no slowing down...and no turning back.

The PsychoZone series by David Lubar

❏ **Kidzilla & Other Tales**
0-812-55880-4 $4.99/$6.50 CAN

❏ **The Witch's Monkey & Other Tales**
0-812-55881-2 $3.99/$4.99 CAN